# THE HOLIDAYS WITH DR. MITCHELL

## THE BILLIONAIRES' CLUB HOLIDAY ROMANCE SERIES

❄

### RAYLIN MARKS

# CHAPTER 1

❄

Jake

Anyone who knows me, knows I'm the best cardiovascular surgeon (and hottest piece of ass) at world-renowned Saint John's Hospital, and I love every aspect of my job, but that's not even the best part about my life. The best part is that aside from having the career of my dreams, I have the most fantastic wife in the galaxy and the two coolest kids.

My beautiful brunette beauty of a wife is a talented painter and successful gallery owner, and she forever changed my life from the first moment I laid eyes on her. Of course, I didn't realize it at the time, but I'd met my soulmate that fateful day when she spilled her fucking green Matcha Frappuccino all over me. That fiasco led to a dozen decisions that would spell out our amazing future and the dream of a life I'd been living with her since we first met.

Meeting her and unexpectedly falling insanely in love forced my ass to grow up in more ways than one. And now, here I was, one happy-ass mother fucker on his way home, daydreaming about her and the beautiful family we shared.

I wanted for absolutely nothing in life. I was content. I was happy. I was fulfilled.

*Ring! Ring!*

"Sup?" I answered my best friend's call.

"What are you doing?" Collin asked.

"I just left the hospital fifteen minutes ago, as you well know, since I beat you out of the parking lot. What do you think I'm doing?"

"Sitting in traffic."

"Bingo," I said, crawling on the freeway at a snail's pace during rush hour traffic. "I was also daydreaming about how perfect my life is until you called and interrupted me."

"Well, you're not going to think your life is perfect once you hear what our lovely women have planned for our holidays this year."

"It's still October. I know we're not talking about Christmas yet."

"That's what I told Elena when she called me as soon as I left the— *Fucking Shitbird! Get the fuck out of the way, then!*"

I smirked, listening to Collin yell at another commuter who'd sent him to a road rage fit.

"Did you miss your exit?" I laughed.

"Dumb fucking idiot came into my lane where there is *no room*, slammed on the brakes, and—"

"It's called traffic, dipfucker. That's happened to me about fifteen times since you called, but I've kept my mood calm and collected."

"That's only because your wife hasn't yet called you to tell you that you're taking the kids trick-or-treating this year in Aster's cute little suburban neighborhood."

"And she won't call me to tell me that because she knows I would say no," I said, changing lanes, trying to get out of this lock-up, and wishing I had a passenger with me to hit the carpool lane to get my ass home.

"You're so fucked if you think you're getting out of this."

"I don't think, Collin, I know."

"Yeah, well, I just want to know if you'd like to get drunk before or after the Halloween block party we'll be attending a week from Thursday?"

"From the bitch fit you're throwing, I'd advise *you* to drink before *and after.*"

"Pointless talking to you," he said, annoyed because he couldn't weasel out of these things like I could.

"Yeah, probably so. Ash knows I won't be walking around in some rando neighborhood. I'd rather buy the kids candy, put on a cute Halloween flick, and call it a holiday."

"Let me know what you're dressing up as," Collin said, ignoring my self-assuredness.

"Dressing up as? Collin, I'm not doing this shit. If anything, I'll be at work. Trick-or-treating is for the moms, not the dads."

"Is that so?" I heard my wife's voice hauntingly chime through my car's intercom, leading me to glance around for sight of her.

"Ash?"

"Yes, my love. It's me…the *mom.*"

"When did you jump on the call?" I asked.

"I added *you* to my call with Ash after I called her to tell her to convince Elena to change the plans," Collin chuckled, knowing the words I'd confidently stated were overheard by the woman who would make sure I was humbled by them.

"Goddamn you, Col," I said, rolling my eyes.

"This is how it's going to go down, Jacob," my wife continued, using the name my older brother loved to call me by when he was chomping into my ass for not doing things in his proper, CEO way. "We *moms* will be hosting a haunted house in John and Mickie's garage, handing out candy and entertaining the trick-or-treaters who come to the house. While we're enjoying ourselves, kicking back with a bottle or three of wine, you *dads* will walk the kids through the neighborhood, going house-to-house and enjoying all the fun memories that come with trick-or-treating."

*Nice guilt trip.*

"Ash, why are we making a big deal out of this holiday?" I asked, kind of shocked that we were even having this conversation. "Your spirit guides must be very disappointed."

I smiled, knowing I could use my wife's hippie mentality to tease her.

I heard Collin chuckling on the other end of the line and decided right then that I would probably kick his ass tomorrow for this shit.

"We aren't doing seances, lover. I'm sure they'll be just fine," she teased.

"If you say so," I answered her. "Okay, fine. I won't fight you on this, but only if you make Collin—"

"Collin is going, Jake," Ash interrupted. "Elena has sworn he will face a year-long dry spell if he doesn't."

"A year-long dry spell for missing out on Halloween?" I answered, baffled about why the gals were coming in so hot on this, as if it was a plan for Christmas morning festivities.

"Yes. You *dads* always find excuses to work or be out of town every year on these holidays because you think they aren't as important as Christmas or *your birthdays*. This year, all that changes. You'll all be doing the heavy lifting with smiles on your faces."

"You have *your boy* to thank for this, you know?" Collin said. "It was little John who insisted we dads help out the moms every once in a while."

"That boy is too smart for his own good sometimes," I rolled my eyes. "All right, I'm down for doing this, but we all have to go one hundred percent," I said, excited to punish Collin for this shit show that made the traffic I was stuck in seem like paradise. "We all dress up in costumes."

"Done," Collin said too happily and quickly.

"But you can't be your profession, bitch," I reacted to his smug excitement. "No doctors."

"I'm not going to a fucking costume store, no. I have no idea what I'd even do?"

"Come up with something. I mean, you acted like a dick by privately having my wife listen to this call and busting my balls as you

THE HOLIDAYS WITH DR. MITCHELL

did, so why don't you get a fuck-ton of rubber and dress up like the dildo we all know you are."

"You think it's going down like this, eh?" Collin said, and now my wife was laughing on the line.

"You two *children* figure out what you're dressing up as. I need to get Kaley out of her bath and ready for bed."

"Love you, baby. I'll be home in about thirty if I ever get out of this traffic," I said.

"Love you too," she hung up after she said goodbye.

"And Collin? Shit just got real."

"Oh, you want to be a dick to me like this is all *my* idea?" he said.

"No, honey," I teased. "You're about to find out why you don't fuck with me when it comes down to trick-or-treating all night with a bunch of crazy little candy addicts."

"We'll see about that."

We ended the call, and the challenge to make everyone's life interesting on Halloween had begun to excite me. Collin thought he was being cute, but he must've forgotten that I thrive in conditions where I get to retaliate against those I love most. This situation would easily afford me that opportunity.

# CHAPTER 2

❄

Ash

W ell, I suppose there was nothing like pissing off my husband after he'd had a long day at the hospital. Ultimately, I wanted him to be more present with me and our children, but I didn't want to go at it like I had with Collin's sneaky three-way call.

After being married to the man for nine years, I learned that nothing ever went as planned with my husband. Once Collin was thrown into the mix, I should've guessed how it would go. Those two tended to act like three-year-olds throwing temper tantrums whenever they were asked to do more to help their wives. It wasn't like Jake and I were growing apart; I just missed him. So, when the ladies and I got together for lunch yesterday, I was grateful to find that I wasn't the only one missing my husband while juggling parental responsibilities and navigating married life.

It was all very typical, but with our men, it seemed that if we didn't ask them—or *mandate* them—to be present and part of things more often, they'd think everything was okay and continue on like nothing was wrong.

I'd learned a long time ago with Jake that he never intentionally tried to avoid family things like Halloween or birthdays for the kids and such. Still, since his absence bothered me, I needed to communicate that I wanted my husband to be a part of these things. If he didn't know, he would think everything was fine—simple communication 101. Regardless, I didn't intend to smear it in his face like I felt I had done after that phone call.

Honestly, I'd had plenty of nights like I was having tonight where I missed dressing sexy for my husband when I knew he'd be home by seven if traffic were clear. I loved looking beautiful for him—desirable to him—but I was far from that tonight.

I was just in a funk. I wore boxer shorts and an oversized shirt, and my usual wavy hair was frizzy and controlled by the damp ocean breeze. I didn't meditate this morning like I always did first thing in the morning, and since the sun never broke through this damn moist fog that loomed over the ocean just beyond the back of our beach house, I concluded that combination was a significant contributor to my mood.

"Hey, monster," I heard Jake say. "Where's your momma, and why aren't you in bed?"

"I wanted you to say good night to me, Daddy," I heard our daughter, who was just as mischievous as her dad, say. "And tell me a story."

"You got it, sis," he said. "But first, where's John? I have a bone to pick with your brother. Then we'll do bedtime stories."

"Was traffic bad?" I questioned, walking out to my handsome man, who couldn't look like shit if he tried. "Or did you sit in the driveway until nine, crying over having to take the kids trick-or-treating?"

"Daddy's taking us trick-or-treating?" Kaley questioned with excitement.

"I am now that you're aware of it, my little bug. Now, where's John?"

"I'm right here, Dad, and I'm too old for bedtime stories."

I smiled, always amused by how our eight-year-old son loved challenging his father like he was the adult in the relationship.

Jake set Kaley back on the ground after squeezing her tight and giving her smooches on her chubby, three-year-old cheeks.

"You're too old for bedtime stories, eh?" Jake arched a challenging eyebrow at him.

"Yup," John said. "I need to go to bed and—"

"Well, I'm too old to dress up for Halloween and take you trick-or-treating, wise guy."

John smiled, "Ha, you have to dress up?"

"I don't *have* to do anything. I *want* to."

"What are you going to be?" John questioned, his excitement growing with the knowledge that his dad would be a part of our Halloween festivities.

"I'm not sure yet, but you know your dad. I'll be the coolest one dressed for Halloween, kid."

"Is Uncle Collin dressing up, too?" John questioned.

"Yes," I answered.

"Then you won't be the coolest," John said.

"No way. Uncle Collin will be," Kaley confirmed with a chipper giggle.

"You kids only think he'll be cooler because he spoils both of you," Jake rolled his eyes dramatically. "He won't be better than me. Trust me."

"It's time for bed," I said. "It's past nine, and we all have to be up by six in the morning."

"And your poor, old dad has surgery early, that means I need to wake up at four in the morning," Jake said while I internally sighed.

I just wanted to have more time with him. We had so many nights like this where he got home late and slept only a few hours before he had to get up and do it all again. I missed the old Jake and me. I hated feeling like this because most doctors who lived an hour away from the hospital would just sleep there if they had to be up at four for surgeries the next day. I was grateful that Jake always came home to us, but those efforts weren't enough tonight.

"Do you want me to read to them?" I questioned.

"No," Jake took Kaley's hand. "We'll do a quick bedtime story, then it'll be light's out, Mom."

"Okay," I said, turning and allowing this negative vibe to follow me into the bedroom. I took the decorative pillows off the bed and turned to go wash my face, brush my teeth, and prep for bed, praying that this rotten mood would be gone in the morning.

"HEY, BABY," Jake said, his strong hands running up each side of my legs. "Your sexy ass is *not* going to sleep until I have my way with you."

"I'm far from sexy," I admitted.

"Don't ever speak lies about yourself like that," he said, his voice low.

"Well, I don't feel sexy," I said, hating that I was in this pathetic mood.

Jake's lips touched my neck while he pulled my oversized tee shirt over my head. "Then it's time I make my wife feel on the inside the way she is on the outside. You're beyond sexy, baby. You're fucking gorgeous, and you're going to know that very well when I'm finished with you."

His lips and tongue ran down the center of my spine, his hands cupping my breasts before moving down to remove my shorts and underwear. I grinned when his teeth gently nipped each of my ass cheeks, and then he turned me to face him. I looked down, tears filling my eyes with so much love and gratitude for this man who always made me feel beautiful, even on my worst day.

I cradled his face in my hands, smiling down into his deep blue eyes that were peering up at me with a love that made me feel like his queen.

"I love you, Jacob Mitchell," I said. "You are the best man."

He rose and carried me to our bed with ease. "The kids are down, and I don't care if I go to sleep late tonight."

"But your surgery?"

"Stop making excuses for your grown-ass man of a husband. *You* are my priority, angel. Tomorrow's surgery should not be on your mind because, I assure you, it's not on mine."

Being loved by a husband who knew how to meet not only your sexual needs but your emotional needs as well was something all wives wanted. I was so thankful I didn't have to ask him for this or that I didn't have to complain about my shitty day for him to make me feel beautiful again.

Jake just knew. He always seemed to know what I needed without me ever saying a word. I was blessed beyond all measure to have this man in my life, and even with my battle with cancer, he'd proved himself to be ten million times the husband I could've ever asked for, helping me get through that terrifying time not just physically, but mentally as well.

I was a very blessed woman, and I was so happy the funk that'd followed me throughout the day was nonexistent now.

# CHAPTER 3

❄

Jake

If there was one thing I didn't take for granted in life, it was my wife and the love we shared. Before Ash, I was a mess on every level. She was my other half and made me a better man in more ways than one.

So, when I came home from work to find the love of my life looking so worn out, sad, and seemingly depressed, everything within me went to work to ensure her worries were dissolved. I understood my wife carried a heavier burden than I did, working in her gallery and lovingly fulfilling our children's every need while simultaneously being the ideal wife. Though I had no idea what got my lady down today, I could only imagine it was because she felt lonely. Being married to a surgeon called for quite a few days and nights of being alone, and that wasn't including all the times I was unexpectedly called away in the middle of spending time together because of emergencies.

Regardless of the reasons for her sad and worn expression, the simple fact was that my angel needed affection and love, and I was the man to give that to her.

Hearing her soft whimpers and feeling my hair being gripped in her fists while I was devouring the delicious taste of her hot sex was turning my ass on, and I was craving more. While Ash laid her head back into the pillows, her legs fell open wider, and her hips arched up, allowing me more access to the one part of her body that I loved bringing to heights of pleasure the way I knew I could.

My hands gripped each side of her waist while I used my lips and tongue to massage her clit. While Ash's grip tightened at the back of my head, she covered her mouth with her other hand, muting the sounds of arousal she was experiencing. Her ass moved higher in the air, her heels dug into the bed, and she pressed my head harder into her delicious pussy.

"Like that, baby," she called out breathlessly in a whisper.

It was pretty humorous how we had to whisper so we wouldn't bring attention to the kids sleeping upstairs. Sometimes it was frustrating as fuck for me because I wanted to hear her scream in pleasure, but if that happened, our kids would be traumatized for life.

I buried my tongue in her opening, seeing she was dripping wet and riding the edge like my angel always did before she found her release of pleasure.

"Come all over my face, angel," I said, begging to taste more of her.

"I love you," she whined. "I need you inside me."

Her voice trailed off, and her wish was my command. If there was one thing I learned a long time ago while having sensational sex with my wife, it was to follow her lead and do as she said. If she wanted to come solo, she would. If her pleasure consisted of my dick being buried inside her, then that's what happened. Playing control-sex games in bed with my lady was never something I did.

I had my clothes off in record time and my dripping wet cock moving in her to match what her soft moans were telling me. Ash didn't want this hard and fast. She wanted me to move slowly against her G-spot.

She was so fucking wet and tight while she held back her release.

The heat from her made my cock jolt with a need to come, but I held back, allowing the tension to build. While I moved my length in and out of her slowly, feeling her pussy contracting around me, she framed my face with her hands while I brought my hungry mouth to her hard nipples. Fuck, I loved her breasts. I could be here all day, massaging my dick in my wife's pussy while gently sucking her perfect tits.

Ash moaned in satisfaction, her climax on the brink while she fell into a trance of desire.

"God, you're perfect," I stated truthfully.

She moaned in gratitude as we fell into a harmonic rhythm of balance and pleasure as we always had. It was as if our bodies and minds knew precisely what the other needed, and when we both entered the drunken sex stupor of ecstasy, our minds could shut off, and our bodies would absently take over.

I needed her lips, and that's where I set my focus next, kissing her deeply and passionately while allowing my cock to pleasure her at this moment. Ash's fingers weaved through my hair again, and I began moving in and out of her faster. She reached for her clit, and our eyes met, knowing that we needed this release right now. In perfect harmony, our bodies and souls dancing in glorious passion, our eyes locked, and the coiled-up energy that had been ready to release my cum deep into my beautiful angel was here.

I moved deeper and faster, following her lead and feeling so fucking phenomenal that I could do this all night long. Ash's body tensed with mine, and then we released the pent-up energy we'd worked to build up to the moment.

I smiled, watching Ash's eyes glaze over in ultimate relaxation. Her lazy smile told me she felt satiated and as beautiful again as I always knew her to be.

"You've still got it, Jacob Mitchell," she said, kissing me on my nose.

"And I plan to still have it well into my nineties," I chuckled.

"Nineties?" she softly laughed. "You know very well that if you and I are fortunate enough to live to our nineties, John and Kaley will have us both thrown into a nursing home and then what will you do?"

"Fuck you in the nursing home; what else would I do?"

"Oh, please. We'll both be old and in diapers," she said, kissing me on the top of my head.

"Fuck that shit. Even if we were, I'd slide your diaper off and—"

"Stop, stop," she interrupted me. "I don't need any visuals of that."

"You're the one challenging me. The point is that it doesn't matter how old we get. I will always want you as much as I have since the day we first met. Besides, ninety is the new fifty. I plan to look just as sexy at ninety as I do now."

"Fine, I'll let you have that. I mean, look at my dad and Carmen. They're in their seventies and look like they're in their fifties."

"And your dad is tapping that ass—"

"Don't you dare!" she covered her face with both hands. "I don't want to think about my dad and Carmen."

I loved seeing Ash like this, happy and silly, and all the stresses of life have gone from her mind. It was just like old times.

"You're the one giving me visuals of you in a rest home wearing diapers."

"You gave that visual to yourself," she arched a playful eyebrow at me, then traced her fingers across my forehead. "Diapers or not, I will forever love you."

"Me too, angel, and I'm sorry if you had a bad day. I hate seeing sadness on your beautiful face."

She rolled her eyes while I rolled onto my side, bringing her to face me. I ran my hand over her perfect ass and continued to gently run my fingertips up her side, along her shoulder, and back down to her ass again.

Pillow talk was my favorite part of marriage. Some men hated it, but I loved this shit, listening as my lady opened up to me about her day, her naked body pressed into mine, and her vibrant and happy eyes dancing with excitement to tell me all about it.

"It was just a dull day. I think the gloomy weather got to me."

"I figured your cute ass would've been all songs and dances when I walked in that door tonight, knowing you and Elena were victorious in mandating that Collin and I go trick-or-treating this year."

"It's not just you two, you know?"

I smiled, wondering who else would be forced into this bullshit.

"Do tell. I'd like to know who else is just as fucked as us two screwballs."

She grinned, "I think it'll be more fun for all of you guys to get on your silly group chats and bitch to each other about it."

"Well, it seems Collin was the first to find out since he's the only one I've heard from."

"The rest will start flooding in soon, I'm sure," she laughed, curled into me, and kissed my chest. "Thank you for tonight. I needed you and that more than you know."

I pulled her in closer and allowed our bodies to mold into each other before I called for my phone to set the morning alarm and kissed Ash on her forehead.

"Don't ever thank me for that, angel. It's always my pleasure to bring a smile to your face. Now, sleep."

It was the last thing she and I said to each other before I drifted off into a much-needed and welcomed slumber.

# CHAPTER 4

Jake

O f all the weeks I would've loved to have time slow down, it would've been this one; however, shit wasn't going down that way, so I chose to take control of the situation instead of letting it steer me into a negative mood.

Acting like a little bitch that all of us *dads* were tasked with the duties of taking toddlers through John and Mickie's neighborhood to knock on doors and say trick-or-treat all damn night wasn't going to get me anywhere, so I figured I would make the most of it. I decided that if I was going trick-or-treating, I was going to be the best-dressed son of a bitch out there.

When I learned that my brother Jim and his best friend Alex were dressing up as Batman and Robin, I chose to steer clear of superheroes altogether, especially since my eight-year-old was the utmost authority on all things Marvel. I'm sure John was going to give Uncle Jim and Alex a fuck-ton of shit for choosing DC characters, and I wasn't about to be part of that lecture, so I decided on a costume that would dominate in all our adorable little daughters' eyes. Even my son would stand in awe of the costume I picked to parade these turkeys through the neighborhood.

I'd probably be the last guy to show up tonight since work held me over, and I had to rush home to get my costume on before driving to *Bungalow Heaven,* where John and Mickie bought an adorable Craftsman to raise their family in. It was the perfect place for two doctors who wanted to escape the loud and busy life of the rich and famous and live like the stars of Leave it to Beaver.

Once I pulled into where we were instructed to park, I hiked my ass up to the Aster family home, not failing to notice the charm of their neighborhood. It was cute as fuck at Halloween. Every lawn and house was decorated with a charming Halloween theme, and neighbors waved from chairs planted on their front lawns as I strutted my ass up the street, looking for the abode that John and Mickie called home.

"What the hell kind of a geek did *you* dress up as?" I heard Spencer Monroe say with humor.

"The one who will win the hearts of our little ladies," I confidently grinned, clapping my hand on the shoulder of my brother's VP at Mitchell and Associates. "Why aren't you dressed up?"

"By the time I'd flown in from business overseas, and *after* this charade was announced mandated by our scheming wives, no more costumes in the store would fit me. Well, none that I would wear, anyway. So, I was left with no other option but to—"

"Does Nat know you didn't dress up?" I interrupted his cocky diatribe.

"After Natalia called to inform me that I had to take our daughter trick-or-treating and that she has a late, last-minute showing, I knew I'd get out of it. In fact, I predicted this would happen, and here we are."

"Well, you don't matter either way," I said. "Angel is, what, a little over a year old? She wouldn't remember the holiday if you begged her to."

"She just had her second birthday, but I do agree. She won't remember any of this—" Spencer cut himself off mid-sentence, and his eyes were the size of silver dollars, looking at something behind me.

My eyes went to Jim, who'd just walked out of the house and immediately covered his smile with his hand.

"Jesus Christ. What the fuck is that?" Alex declared with humor as he exited behind Jim. Their Batman and Robin costumes were full-blown cosplay level, so I had to give it to them.

They still looked like idiots, though.

"It's Spencer's costume," I heard Nat say from behind me.

I didn't want to turn to look at what she held because the expression on Spencer's face and the men walking out of John and Mick's house were priceless to behold, but I was too curious not to. Once I caught a glimpse of the costume Natalia was holding, all I knew was that I was thankful she was not *my* spouse.

"Big bird?" Spencer said with baffled disgust. "That thing is ludicrous, and I'm shocked you even allowed it in your damn car."

We all remained silent, watching Spencer living the nightmare that the cocky bastard deserved.

"Well, it is your daughter's favorite character on Sesame Street, so you *will* strut your handsome ass around in this."

"This whole trick-or-treat idea that you ladies have devised is beyond my comprehension," Spencer said. "I'm not wearing that shit. I will take Angel to a couple of houses, and that's it. Why aren't you at your showing?"

"Do not speak to me as if I'm some child, Spencer Monroe," she seethed. "In fact, this *idea* of ours was all mine because I'm sick of you always missing these events. You're always overseas," she looked at Jim, "and always working. Missing Angel's second birthday was where I drew the line, honey," she smirked, and Spencer crumbled. "Now, before you make yourself look more foolish in front of your friends, I suggest you put the costume on and be the father of the year. Actions are speaking much louder than words tonight, gentlemen." She eyed us before looking me up and down and laughing, "What the hell are you, a geek?"

"Geek? No, Nat. The yellow ball of feathers with orange plastic legs you're about to drop your husband into is the *geek* costume of the night."

"His daughter's opinions and mine are all that matters," she shrugged. "And Big Bird is our favorite."

"I'll say," Jim dared to speak while Nat was in the process of ripping everyone a new one.

"Dad?" I heard John say as he walked out of the house. He was dressed as Iron Man and all the kids were following him around like he really was Tony Stark. "Why are you dressed like Harry Potter?"

"He's every kid's favorite at your age, and your mother loves him, too. Did I nail this or what?"

"Your cape is too short, your hair is way too perfectly styled, and your wand looks like you made it from paper straws."

"Leave it to your boy to critique his favorite character," my brother said with a laugh. "You would've done well to dress up as Loki and be his enemy for the night."

John grinned, "Am I being too hard on you, Dad?"

"Just a little," I said, shrugging my shoulders and feeling sorry for myself that my kid didn't think I was amazing.

"I think it's cool," he said.

"I don't need your pity, boy," I taunted him.

"I know, but I'm glad you're here, and it's cool you dressed up as one of my favorite book characters."

Back on the high-status train, my ego was fed, and I was all smiles and cockiness again.

"The best thing about little John, aside from sharing the same name as me, is that he keeps your arrogance in check. Have any of you guys seen my wife?" John Aster said, stepping out onto his front porch where we all stood.

"Yeah, thanks, Aster," I said. "I haven't seen Mick, but I just got here, and then I got blinded by Big Bird, so I'm not sure where she is."

"Seb and Darcy needed a hand to encourage Charlotte to trick-or-treat tonight," Jim said. "I imagine Charlotte is still struggling with her transition to living in California."

"Poor thing," Alex said. "I can't imagine growing up so isolated and then being thrown into the midst of all of us. Her anxiety must be soaring."

"Well, I know the ladies will work together to help her. I mean, if Seb's daughter digs Big Bird, then she'll be living the high life once Spencer is dressed for this occasion."

As I expected, my Harry Potter impersonation won the hearts of everyone. After we got our laughs at Spencer's expense out of the way, we allowed Big Bird to take the lead with his daughter, his fat, feathery ass waddling as we began walking toward the end of the driveway at dusk.

The sun had begun to set, and the sky was painted a beautiful orange hue, perfectly fitting the occasion in this charming neighborhood on this particular night. Collin's dumbass got held up at work, so that fucker actually got completely out of this whole shindig, but who cared? He'd hate to be riding second best to me, and that was a fact.

When we turned up the sidewalk to head to our first house, I couldn't believe my eyes.

"Whoa!" Addy, Jim's oldest daughter, said. "That's so awesome!"

"It's like at Disneyland," John said.

"Damn, that is pretty freaking incredible," Jim added.

I stood in awe of the Headless Horseman, trotting up the street towards us with a lit pumpkin in his hand. Somehow, this person had rigged a smoke machine to the saddle, creating the most badass effect.

"John and Mick's neighborhood knows how to go out of their way to make this one hell of an event," Alex said.

Everyone on the street stood and watched as the Headless Horseman began galloping toward us.

"Who's that?" Spencer said.

I swear to God, I would never be able to lose the image of Spence in this damn costume.

"Neighborhood watch, I assume," Jim said.

The horse trotted directly up to where Collin's little son, Alex, held onto Logan and Albert Grayson's hands protectively. My son nutted up immediately and went over to the little boys as the Headless Horseman started to give even me an eerie vibe.

It took Izzy and Kaley running to my brother for protection for the Headless Horseman to pull open the cloak that was hiding his head.

"It's just me," Collin said with a cheerful grin.

I glared at my best friend, and his challenging smirk and arched eyebrow landed on me.

"Are you fucking with me right now?" I said. "Really? You brought a goddamn horse into this?"

Standing there as the children gasped and fawned all over Collin's costume made me realize I looked no cooler than Big Bird, and Collin flashed a Cheshire Cat grin at me.

"Harry Potter, eh? How very original," he said. "Better pay some respect, bitch."

"There are kids here. Watch your language," I stated, trying to bring this man's ego down a few octaves.

"When has that ever stopped us?" he truthfully asked.

"Never," Jim interjected while Sebastian finally caught up to us, holding Charlotte, dressed as Princess Ariel, in his arms. "In fact, because of your and Jake's usual shenanigans, I was shocked we were all trusted to be alone with these kids and *not* ruin their holiday."

"It's okay," my all-knowing snitch of a son said as he looked at Jim, "My mom already told me to expect that my dad and Collin would be in a costume war, and because of that, they'd curse all night."

"Smart one, your mom," Jim said to my son. "Then, we won't have to worry about bad examples being set tonight."

The thing about us group of assholes, especially Collin and me, was that we knew how to have a damn good time. We were making memories with our kids, and that's all that mattered. Even though Collin's costume had me beat by a hundred miles, our kids would never forget the *one* night their fathers dressed up and walked them through Bungalow Heaven in Pasadena.

The best part was knowing that putting in all this work got us off the hook for the rest of the holidays. We all nailed it, even Spencer, whose ass was wagging up the street to the sounds of Collin's horse's hooves. All of this was unforgettable, and our ridiculous egos rounded it out perfectly.

# CHAPTER 5

✳

Ash

"How was school, John?" I asked as John slid into the backseat next to his sister, who was overly thrilled to pick her brother up from school.

"I got an A on my math test," he said with his usual air of arrogance.

I smiled at him as I pulled out of the school parking lot. I waved at Mrs. Thomas, the school principal, as she helped guide students to their buses. Someone had to keep the kids safe from all the parents who were always in a frenzy, waiting in the car line to get their kids from the pickup lane.

"Your dad will be happy to hear that. You were stressed about this one, though," I said. "Are you sure you want to keep taking advanced classes?"

I smirked when I glanced up and saw John roll his eyes through the rearview mirror, "Dad didn't become one of the youngest chief cardiologists in the country because he screwed off in school. He took advanced classes and didn't stop until he reached the top."

I sighed. "That is true; however, your dad said he wasn't being challenged enough, so his father insisted he take gifted classes. You don't have to do that. You can still be successful in anything you do without putting pressure on yourself like that."

"I know, Mom," he nodded, but my advice was falling on deaf ears.

Jake and I had very different upbringings when it came to academics. I was an artist, and my parents had always nurtured that side. Jake, however, was raised by his father, who pressured him to excel in everything, which wasn't surprising when I thought about it. His father was the founding CEO of Mitchell and Associates, and it took tremendous drive and dedication to run such a global empire. Jake and Jim's father wanted his sons to succeed in their own right, not just be trust-fund babies who ran around living off their daddy's money. His plan ultimately worked since Jim went on to take over as CEO of the company, and Jake had gone on to have a distinguished career as a cardiovascular surgeon, becoming chief at a world-renowned hospital as a young man.

The difference with John was that I didn't want my son to think he needed to take the same path as his father just to prove that he could be successful. I wanted John to do whatever he was passionate about. Maybe I was getting ahead of myself, though. After all, he was only eight.

As I contemplated John's schoolwork, Kaley drifted off to sleep in her car seat, and John put in his earbuds, most likely trying to avoid any further conversation of me trying to coach him along.

*Ring! Ring!*

"Hey, Avery," I answered the car phone. "What's up?"

"Girl," she said with the dramatic annoyance she usually held when her daughter, Addison, was arguing with their youngest, Isabel. "We need a goddamn vacation."

"Honey, you're always on vacation," I laughed. "I know so because I'm usually babysitting for you when Jim whisks you away to your castle in England."

"I mean a girl's vacation. Just the ladies," she said.

"Is Jim irritating you?" I laughed.

"No more than usual," she chuckled. "I don't know what it is. I'm just at my limit. I'm sick of hearing Izzy and Addy fighting nonstop and Jim pacing the floors every time a deal goes sideways. I'm just burnt."

"I heard that big merger didn't go through, which surprised me because Spence thought he had that thing nailed down."

"The whole thing was a bust after they found out about that company's embezzlement shit," she confirmed. "It's all good now, but days like this make me want to get away with my girls."

"We can always steal the yacht and leave the kids with Carmen and my dad?" I teased.

"Why don't we meet for coffee tomorrow? I miss you, and the two of us haven't hung out by ourselves in forever. I want to have coffee at a cute little hole-in-the-wall diner on the beach and watch the sunrise."

"That sounds awesome," I said, feeling Avery return to reality again. "There's an adorable coffee shop and bookstore down by my gallery that's cozy inside and out. I'll see how early they open."

"Why haven't I heard about this little gem before?" Avery questioned with a laugh.

"Because, like you said, it hasn't been just you and me in a long time. We're forever doing dinner dates with our husbands, or I'm trying to soak up my rare time alone with Jake."

"We can't let marriage kick our asses like this," Avery said. "Seriously. We're getting caught up in the trap of the mundane."

"We're just living our lives with our husbands and kids," I chuckled. "Shit, you must've had a really shitty day."

"It's been rough. I'm dealing with a frustrating woman in my clinic. It's hard because we all love her and understand the situation she's in with her marriage and the abuse, but every time she leaves the guy, he speaks these big, beautiful words to her, and she falls for it. It's a tale as old as time, I guess. After all these years, I shouldn't be surprised, but it gets to me every time."

I frowned. Avery founded a women's shelter to help those looking to leave domestic violence situations, hoping to help them start over and providing a safe space and numerous resources. I was so proud of her and her work because I couldn't imagine how difficult it must've been to pour out all that love and support daily, constantly trying to help others.

"Okay, after I get home, I'll look the place up. If nothing else, we can do lunch. I will be at the gallery tomorrow anyway while Carmen and my dad take Kaley to the museum for the day, so it'll be perfect."

"Sweet. Love you, Ash," she said.

"You too, babe," I said, and then we hung up.


I STOOD BEFORE THE STOVE, stirring the Bolognese sauce I'd made to prepare John and Kaley's favorite meal. They loved spaghetti, and when their dad worked his 48-hour shifts at the hospital, we cooked the food he despised. I still couldn't believe Jake hated spaghetti. He always acted like it was equal to eating dog food.

Oh, well. It was truly his loss because my sauce was delicious, so he could suck it.

"Momma?" I heard Kaley say, her voice sounding like she had a stuffy nose.

After placing the garlic parmesan bread in the oven to broil, I turned, "Yeah, baby? Dinner will be done in about ten minutes, so go wash up and tell your brother."

"I'm scared," she said.

I turned to see her glassy eyes filled with a bit of panic, "What did John say to you now? Halloween is over, and so is the time for spooky stories."

"I can't breathe in my nose," she said.

"What do you mean?" I walked over to her, seeing her nose and sinuses oddly swollen.

I pressed around, feeling hard nodules in her nose, and then I tilted her head back.

"Ow, Mommy," she said while I pinched my lips to avoid laughing at this wildly unexpected turn of events.

"You have a jellybean stuck in your nose, silly," I said, gently pushing on her nose, and a green jellybean dropped out of it.

She started crying. "There's more," she said with embarrassment.

"More?" I said. "How many more?"

"A lot," she said. "They hurt."

"Good God," I said, a little fearful now. I felt around and tried to push down from the outside, but I had no idea what I was dealing with and didn't want to hurt her. "Do you know how many are in there?"

"I can't count, Mommy. Remember?"

I sat back on my heels, trying to contemplate what the hell to do.

*Right! Cameron. He's in pediatrics.*

"Hold on. Let me call Cam and see what he thinks. Maybe he can come over and help." Jesus H. Christ. The joys of unexpected surprises from a three-year-old. "Hey, Ash," Jessa, Dr. Brandt's wife, answered on the first ring. "What's up, lady?"

"Hey, honey. I'm sorry to bug you at dinner time, but Kaley decided to shove beans up her nose. I have no idea how many are in there, and I was wondering if I should take her into Saint John's or if Cam was home and could help me with this?"

The Brandts lived close to us in Malibu, and since Cam was a softie, I knew he wouldn't be put out to come over and free my daughter's sinuses from jellybean prison.

"Cam's on-call tonight, so just take her in, and he'll be the one to treat her."

"Thanks so much, honey. I'll do that," I said, annoyed to be heading to the hospital instead of eating spaghetti.

That's when the smoke detector started blaring a notification that my goddamn garlic bread had caught on fire and my pot of noodles was boiling over everywhere.

Dear God, why did things escalate into disastrous affairs with no warning? I'd gone from peacefully cooking dinner, excited to have coffee on the beach with my best friend, to the full-blown chaos of nasal-cavity jellybeans and a small-scale kitchen fire.

"Grab your coat and get Kaley's, too. We've got to go to the hospital," I hollered at John as he came rushing into the kitchen disapprovingly. "Your sister decided to do some weird experiment by shoving beans up her nose, and I have no idea how many are up there."

"Kaley, you're so weird," John stated with annoyance.

"Be nice, young man. She's scared."

"I'm not weird," Kaley insisted, erupting into a fit of tears.

"You're not weird, Kaley," I said, throwing the charred garlic bread into the sink and spraying it down to keep the damn things from bursting into flames. I shut off all the burners, and the Momzilla in me erupted when I turned to see that John was not doing what I asked while Kaley began crying uncontrollably.

"Everyone stop it this instant," I demanded in a firm voice. "John," I looked at him with an intensity I only had when I was frustrated and pissed off, "go and do as I told you—no arguments and no insults— and meet me and Kaley in the car." I looked at Kaley, "Don't worry. Uncle Cam is going to help get those things out of your nose. Let's go."

# CHAPTER 6

❋

Ash

We sat in the pediatric waiting room, waiting for Dr. Cameron Brandt to come in and relieve my daughter's sinuses. What a damn mess this all was. The nurse finished taking Kaley's vitals and getting our story for Cameron's charts, and God only knew what that man would say when he walked in here.

"I'm hungry," Kaley said, bringing my attention to where she sat, playing with her favorite doll that John had managed to snag before we rushed out of the house.

I smiled at my daughter, amused by how things with kids always went sideways so fast and thankful that things weren't worse.

"Why don't you pull the jellybeans out of your nose and eat them, then?" John smarted off.

"John, focus on your homework," I said, nodding at the iPad he brought.

"Well, I'm just stating the obvious," he said, constantly needing to get in the last word.

"Thank you for that," I said before looking at Kaley, whose expression showed deep shame. "After Cam helps us get those things out of your nose, we'll get something to eat on the way home."

"McDonald's?" she questioned with excitement.

"You know Mommy doesn't like to eat fast food," I said. "Addy needs to stop encouraging you to like that place."

"But it's *yummy*," she said with a cute and devious expression inherited from her dad.

"So is, or *was*, the spaghetti I was making for dinner tonight," I countered.

"By the time Cameron gets in here and treats Kaley, McDonald's will be the only place still open," John said with annoyance, eyeing his sister in reprimand for all of this.

"You'd better watch that attitude, pal," I said with an arch of my eyebrow, having had enough of his attitude. "I'm sure that when Kaley shoved the jellybeans up her nose, she didn't plan on ending with a visit to the hospital. Things happen, so take it easy."

"Okay," he reluctantly agreed, but he was probably internally rolling his eyes. Little shit.

I heard two quick knocks on the door before it cracked open, and Cam came in with the pediatric ER nurse. Cameron was a doll, always leading with his big blue eyes and a bright smile that made you want to smile, too. His dark navy scrub cap had penguins all over it, matching his cheerful and fun personality. No person on earth was more suited to work with sick kids than Cam.

"Hey guys," he said. He saw John sitting in the chair next to the door and ruffled the top of his head before smiling at Kaley and then me, "Quite the night for you, Ash?"

"You can say that again," I said. "Nothing like planning a quiet night at home before the unexpected happens, and here we are."

"Ha," he chuckled, then looked at Kaley, hiding behind her American Girl doll. "Don't tell me your doll shoved jellybeans up her nose, too?"

"No, just me," she said meekly, lowering the doll.

"Well, I have to admit," he sat on his stool and rolled over to where

Kaley sat on the exam table, "I've had many youngsters put jellybeans up their noses, but most of them stop after one. You didn't!"

"No," Kaley admitted, embarrassed.

"Let me guess why," Cam said, tilting her head back to assess the situation, "you wanted to grow a jellybean farm in your nose because your mom and dad won't let you eat all your Halloween candy at once?"

Kaley snort-giggled since she could only breathe through her mouth, making it sound like she was oinking.

"I think that's what happened," the nurse added playfully.

"Hand me the forceps, please, Shelly," Cameron requested. "It's time I start farming this cute little nose and see how many jellybeans we have shoved up there."

"I don't know how many," Kaley said, leaning her head back further while Cameron eased the long tweezers into her tiny nostrils, retrieving the first jellybean.

I watched in humor and disbelief as he continued to pull jellybean after jellybean out of Kaley's nose. I spied John's eyes wide with shock at how many his sister had managed to get up there.

Cam massaged his thumb over her sinuses to ensure they were clear and moved to the other nostril. "Sweetheart, I'm going to give you some advice," he continued to work on her nose, "I know you idolize your dad and Uncle Collin, and I'm fairly confident that is where you got the idea to grow a jellybean farm up your nose, but I'm going to tell you something they don't know," he said while John chuckled.

"Yes?" Kaley said, being perfectly still as Cam searched deeper into her nose for yet another damn jellybean.

"You can't grow candy in your nose," he said as if offering her the wisest advice ever. "I wish you could, but you can't. And now that you know that, we can laugh at Daddy and Uncle Collin when they try this trick."

"It's probably where she got the idea from," I said, feeling relieved this was all pretty much over.

"No," Kaley said, bringing her head back to normal position while

Cameron used his fingers to feel around and see if there were any beans he hadn't managed to find.

"Okay, kiddo. Take a deep breath through your nose and tell me if you can breathe again," Cameron said.

Kaley breathed in deeply and exhaled the biggest sigh of relief I'd ever heard from such a tiny person. "I can breathe in my nose again," she said sheepishly but happily.

"Fantastic," Cam said, nodding toward the nurse who remained silent for most of the procedure. "You're all set, little one. And if your mom's cool with it, we have a basket of toys for you and your brother to grab something from." He looked at John, "And before you smart off, Jim Junior," he said, knowing exactly how John was with *childish things*, "there are some cool footballs and Nerf toys in that basket you might want to consider before you tell me you're too old for toys."

John grinned at Cameron, looking like an eight-year-old for the first time since we arrived at the hospital.

"I'll show you two where the basket is," Shelly said with a friendly smile. "Nice to meet you, Mrs. Mitchell," she added before leaving Cam and me to discuss this craziness and wrap up our visit.

"Thanks, Cam," I said, giving him a hug of relief. "I can't believe we had to come in over this. I can't imagine the hell you'll give Jake."

"Oh, you know how we operate," Cam laughed, "but I don't think tonight is the night to give Jake shit for anything."

"Oh, no," I said, not liking the change in his tone. "Did he lose a patient?"

"Yeah," he nodded. "After Jessa called and told me you were on your way, I tried to get ahold of Jake. I mean, it's obvious that we're hit and miss with availability when working on-call shifts, but Jake just texted back for me to take care of Kaley."

"Damn it," I said, folding my arms and wishing I could be there for my husband right now. "He never does well when he loses someone, even if they aren't a regular patient."

"Dr. Stone was with him. He's the one who told me when I was in the cafeteria getting a coffee. It was a pretty tragic one due to the family's situation. I don't know much, but I'm sure Jake will tell you."

"Well, maybe a little light-hearted humor about what his daughter did tonight will help ease the pain he must be feeling," I said.

"Yeah, probably," he nodded. "I just wanted to let you know. You can go to the cardiac wing and check in. I'll goof around with the kids if you'd like?"

"I'll leave him with his medical team," I said. "I don't want to distract him any more than he already is. I'm thankful you told me, though."

"Not a problem," Cam said, and then the intercom paged Dr. Brandt to an emergency operating room. "It looks like this night is just getting started, and that's my cue." He hugged me quickly, "It's good to see you and the kids, Ash."

"You too, Cam," and with that, Cameron was out the door in a flash.

Being called into a life-saving emergency in the pediatric unit was never a good thing. Nothing was worse than having a sick or injured child, and I hoped to my core that Cameron's patient would be okay. One thing I knew was that whoever was on the table would get the best care available since Cameron was on-call.

It brought to mind Jake's patient and how I'm sure their family didn't wake up this morning and expect to lose a loved one. I suddenly felt overcome with gratitude that the reason for my visit was silly instead of serious. I suppose we all take things for granted when life is going well, especially our health. That was something I'd gotten a crash course in when I found out I had cancer, and it was a lesson I would be remiss to forget.

Tonight, I was grateful that nothing serious had happened to either of my children. I walked out and saw them happily playing with the toys they'd carefully selected from the toy chest, and my resolve not to take them to McDonald's on the way home faded. Why the hell not? A happy meal might be the perfect way to heal jellybean trauma.

# CHAPTER 7

Jake

It'd been a week since my daughter shoved half a dozen jellybeans up her nose, and the fact that I was clocking time by this incident was truly pathetic. I'd gotten a mountain of shit for it from everyone around me, but I expected nothing less.

"Dr. Mitchell," my nurse said, walking through the opened door of my office, "there's a delivery for you?"

I frowned. "Are the monitors I requested finally here?" I questioned.

"It's a bouquet of—"

"Hey gorgeous," Collin said, walking into my office carrying a candy-filled jar wrapped in cellophane with a large blue bow. "Got you a little something since I haven't seen you since you lost the patient last week."

"Thanks, Jackie," I said. "Would you mind keeping an eye out for those monitors? I'm afraid they might end up on the wrong floor."

"No problem. I'll ask admin if they know anything," she said.

"You're the best," I said as she rolled her eyes, waved her hand at me, and walked down the hall.

I looked at Collin, standing there like a party clown who'd come bearing gifts. "Thanks, buddy, but you brought that to the wrong recipient," I said, leaning back in my office chair and running my hands over my face.

I was so fucking tired. I'd felt like this since I lost my patient in the ER the night that Ash brought Kaley in to have Cam extract the jellybeans from her nose.

"Kaley didn't laugh when I told her I had a side business growing candy from my nose," he chuckled and sat in the chair across from my desk.

"Yeah, well, I think she's scarred for life from the total humiliation she suffered after her ER fiasco. You know our kids can't handle being teased and pranked like we can," I said, arching an eyebrow at him.

Collin rolled his eyes and looked up at the ceiling. He seemed to be in a great mood when he walked in, but I'm sure my lack of amusement was taking the wind out of his sails.

"Come on, Jakey. Are you still wearing the G-string Ash likes when you two get kinky, or are you just being a dick because you enjoy it?"

I smiled. "That thong rides up too high when I wear my slacks," I half-laughed, knowing I was just edgy because it had been a long week.

"That's why I wear the lace ones," Jace Stone said, walking into my office with the GQ fashion and charisma that made all the ladies in the hospital follow him around.

"I thought that was because you were thinking about switching teams," Collin said, casually placing an ankle over his knee while Jace took the seat beside him.

"Meh, I'm kicking it around, but men might be too hairy for my taste, and after last night with Michelle Parker? Holy shit," he said, prompting me and Collin to narrow our eyes at his cocky ass.

I smirked, needing this reprieve from my continual overthinking. My work was stressful enough—assessing patient charts, monitoring, performing procedures, and daily stuff that came along with being

Chief of Cardiology—but the stress of losing a patient added on top of that always brought me to the brink.

"You know, when you kiss and tell, you're giving yourself away. You may as well come out and say you've been in a dry spell for months, and you haven't actually been laid in mind-blowing fashion, right?" I said, challenging the young doctor who started working with us at Saint John's close to a year ago.

This eligible bachelor wore his cockiness on his sleeve. He also hadn't yet learned that Collin and I thrived on giving each other hell; we enjoyed it even more when we got to turn it onto someone else who reminded us of who we were before we settled into our married lives and started having our own families.

"Nah, man. It's true," Jace contested.

"Well, it may have been mind-blowing for you, but I doubt it was for her," Collin said.

"I guess you wouldn't know," Jace bantered back.

"Oh, we'd know whether you gave that girl the sexual experience you're in here bragging about," I added.

"I'm not even going to ask," Jace answered, knowing he was walking into the shitshow circus, where Collin and I were proud ringleaders.

"You don't need to because we're going to tell you," Collin continued. "You see, your sexy ass may have it on the operating table, kicking ass and proving to Jake he made an excellent decision to bring you on the team; however, your skills in the bedroom suck."

Jace laughed as I did because of Collin's fake sincerity, trying to sound like a professional sex therapist. I got up and closed my door because I wasn't trying to get all of us reported to HR for trying to be funny when it was entirely inappropriate talk for the workplace. If I weren't in such need of being elevated into a better mood, I would've told Collin to knock it off and save it for the bar, but I needed a good dose of stupidity. John had a band recital tonight, and since I'd already missed too many events, I didn't want to miss this one too. I also didn't want to show up in a lousy mood with a thundercloud over my head.

"Man, you haven't been single for years. You probably forgot how to—"

"You haven't learned when to stop challenging Collin, have you?" I said, chuckling. "Walk away now, and you might still—"

"Too late," Collin interrupted, placing his hand on Jace's shoulder and giving him a devious smile. "This dipfucker has bragged that he doesn't suck in bed," Collin looked at me, "and he thinks we believe him."

"It was just a one-night hook-up," Jace said. "And it doesn't matter if you two dipshits think I was good or not, she did. Her moans and screams proved that."

"You realize women fake that all the time, right?"

"Fake it?" he said with confusion.

"Uh, yeah," Collin said.

"Well, yeah, but why?"

"Why? Because your dick is too small and wasn't doing anything for her," Collin said. "Or maybe you were a selfish bastard trying to get off. Women have a sixth sense, you know? They'll fake it so you can't hold back. Then, after you lose your load, she can go home, shower, and wash the disgusting feeling of *you* off her."

"Uh," Jace muttered, looking like he was recalling the night's events, analyzing all his moves, and wondering if Collin was right.

I couldn't refrain from laughing for busting this player's balls and knocking his ego down several notches.

"Yep," Collin nodded, keeping Jace's paranoia going. "And the reason Jake and I know you sucked is because the receptionists aren't hunting you down to tell you that a woman is harassing them, asking questions about your schedule, demanding to know where you're at, and that kind of thing."

"Oh, God," he said, rolling his eyes. "Your logic is that I sucked in bed because Michelle isn't hunting me down?"

"It's very telling, man," Collin shrugged. "You suck in bed. We don't."

"This is fucked up," Jace laughed, yet it was apparent he was second-guessing whether he was good in bed.

"It's not easy when the one thing you pride yourself on proves to be a failure," I teased. "But thank God you're an amazing surgeon because if you weren't, you wouldn't be able to use your profession to snag unsuspecting minxes like this Michelle character."

"I feel like my job here is done," Collin said, standing up. He looked at Jace, "Next time? I want to see a crazy chick in this office begging for your attention and pissed off about the false promises you made her in bed, or you might as well give it all up."

"You guys can be such dicks," he said with a laugh. "So much so, I forgot why I even walked in here to talk to Jake."

"Finding out you're a sack of shit in bed from your two favorite doctors makes the head spin," Collin looked at the folders that Jace held in his hand. "Edna Marshall and Harold McKinley seem to be the reason you're here to visit the Chief," he said, opening the door and reminding Jace of the charts on our two newest patients. I'd wanted to schedule them for surgery, but I needed to discuss a few things about them with Stone first.

Just as Collin opened the door, Cassidy Blake, one of our front desk administrators who had a serious crush on Stone, was standing there, red in the face, and about to knock on the door.

"Hey, Cass," Collin said. "If you're looking for Dr. Stone, he's in a meeting with Dr. Mitchell."

It was apparent to everyone that Cassidy wanted this man to step out of her dreams and into her car, but sadly, Jace had a lot of learning to do before the man could or would ever settle down, and none of us saw that happening anytime soon. Why else would Collin and I be giving the man so much shit?

"There's a woman at reception asking for you, and she's bothering the staff," she said, looking at Dr. Stone. "Her name is Michelle Parker, and she called a bunch of times demanding to be patched through to you. Levar transferred her to your line, but you weren't in, so she kept calling back, asking him to walk the halls to find you. After Levar told her no for the *sixth time*, she randomly showed up, asking if she could go looking for you herself."

Collin and I looked at each other in shock and humor. Now it was our turn to get shit from Jace about the hell we just gave him. Naturally, Jace looked at us, arching his eyebrow smugly. Great. All we needed was this tall, dark, handsome man strutting around and shoving his peacock feathers in our faces.

"What do you want us to tell her?" Cassidy demanded, obviously hurt that her crush's chick was here, harassing the staff with psychotic urgency.

"Let her know I'll be out in a minute," Jace said, dismissing Cassidy's anger.

He turned to Collin and me, "I'm sorry. What were we just speaking about?"

"Oh, this is a topic for a different day," I said, glancing at my watch. "But you have fun dealing with the one who's planning to boil your bunny if you don't get your sexy ass out there and give her more. As for me, my time is up. I have a recital to be at in thirty minutes, and traffic is already a bitch so let's go over those charts first thing in the morning."

With that, I grabbed my leather briefcase and followed Collin out to see an extremely stunning woman looking like a viper ready to strike, and we couldn't resist grinning at the recollection of our foolish lives before we met our wives. I couldn't count the number of times a full-blown stalker had shown up here and demanded to see me again, insisting she wouldn't be a one-night stand.

"I'm glad those days are over," Collin said as we exited the office buildings, taking the words out of my mouth.

"Makes you feel fortunate to be the happily married men you are, doesn't it?"

"No shit. So, you're not going to Darcy's tonight?"

"The bar?" I asked.

"No, I'm talking about Pride and Prejudice; Fitzwilliam Darcy is expecting you at Pemberley post haste," Collin said sarcastically, rolling his eyes. "Yes, dipshit. I'm talking about the bar."

"Okay, wise-ass," I started, choosing to steer clear of the fact that Collin knew so much about Pride and Prejudice for fear that he'd start talking about it in depth, and I wasn't in the mood to banter about romance novels…for once. "I know your head is up your ass half the time, but we also have a friend named Darcy, you know? And since everyone is on pins and needles, wondering if she and Sebastian will pull the trigger and get a place nearby, I didn't know if that is who you were talking about."

"Seb still has some more ass-kissing to do if you ask me," Collin said.

"Well, didn't we all?"

"Truth. We were all as pathetic as Playboy Stone back there, and if our ladies took us back with a simple sorry, and *I can't live if living is without you* plea, we'd never appreciate the lives we have now."

"Preach," I answered. "Are Seb and Darcy living together?"

"Sort of," Collin said. "From what Elena told me, he bought a place, and she's still officially in Mexico, but I think she's coming back. Who knows?"

"Well, we shall see if he can pull off a miracle. Going dark on Darcy for all those months doesn't get a woman like that to trust so easily again, and I'm damn proud of her strength. I do wish she'd move back, though. Ash adores her."

"We're completely off track and starting to sound like our wives," Collin said. "I felt a lot better about my life talking like bastard assholes with Stone. Anyway, about Darcy's. Jim and everyone else are going to be there. I thought you were going?"

"Dude, it's *the boy's* recital," I said as we approached our cars. "I've missed more than my fair share of shit with my kids over the last year, and the fucking year is almost over. I'm going to have to pass on the testosterone tug fest at the bar, but go with God and enjoy yourself even though all you fuckers should be there supporting John instead of fueling your whiskey addictions."

"Speaking of hitting the bottle, it appears that the ladies aren't stopping at dressing our asses up for trick or treat night. Laney insisted I attend Alex's birthday party with his kindergarten class. And with that came the task of bringing gluten-free, non-dairy cupcakes for all twenty-five kids in attendance and orchestrating games for the kids to play after recess. Not to mention being forced to speak with other parents and chum it up with the teacher—stuff the mothers do, not us."

"Fucking hell," I answered. "This is why I'd better be on time tonight. I'm not fucking Cameron Brandt, and I won't manage to keep my sanity in a room filled with kids."

"Or kids shoving jellybeans up their noses?"

"That's different because it's my kid. I chose to be a doctor and not a teacher for a reason."

Collin grinned, "Well, I'll repeat the exact words my wife used when I gave her the same line of shit to get out of the school room parent shit."

"And they are?" I answered.

"That Elena didn't go to school to be a teacher either, and it's not her favorite thing in the world to be room parent; however, our kids go to this school, and these teachers bust their asses for them. The least we can do is show up and support the teacher, students, and school where our children attend."

"Good God," I answered. "I get that, yes, but seriously? These ladies need to slow down. I'm not trying to be president of the PTA. I'm a surgeon and chief of my ward, and I do my best to show up for my family on my days off. These lessons they're pushing us through are about to get some pushback from me."

Collin chuckled before getting into his car. "Good luck with that, buddy. Whatever you do, don't piss off their aggravated asses even more, or the next thing you know, we'll be cooking Christmas dinner."

With that, Collin and I parted ways, and I felt more irritated than excited to show up at the band recital for my son. I didn't want to have this reaction, but the insinuation that we were a bunch of lazy fucks who were checked out was bothering me.

Regardless of what our wives seemed to think, we were all doing our best, and this pressure to be the perfect father left me with the hollow feeling that I wasn't doing enough.

# CHAPTER 8

❄

Ash

Everyone gave a standing ovation, cheering on the students who performed in tonight's band recital. The kids did a fantastic job, and even though a few students missed a few beats, their hearts were in it, and that's all that mattered.

"Mommy, let's go," Kaley urged, pulling my hand while Mr. and Mrs. Hawthorne greeted me and complimented John's trumpet solo.

John's performance was flawless, and this momma couldn't be prouder of his hard work. He'd practiced diligently for weeks, and it paid off, which made me especially happy since my ears had been ringing for two hours a day while he practiced.

"Hey," I rubbed John's back, reaching down to hold his case after he carefully put away his trumpet. "You were awesome," I said, refraining from embarrassing him by kissing him on the cheek in front of all his peers.

"Thanks, Mom," he said gleefully. This boy was thrilled with himself and his bandmates.

"You were great, John," Ruby Mackey said with a bashful smile.

I grinned at the adorable, dark-haired, green-eyed girl who seemed to have the same crush on John as he had on her.

"Thanks, Ruby," John said.

"Ash, *Mija*," I heard Carmen's voice over the crowd. My sassy and sexy stepmom was one of my favorite people in the world. She was hired as a live-in nurse to care for my dad after his heart attack, and we all fell in love with her, my dad especially.

"Hey, Carmen," I said, smiling at her and Dad as they approached where all the families in attendance stood greeting their kids. "Hi, Dad," I said, welcoming his hug after Carmen had beat him to me and our kids.

"Hey, baby girl. And look at you, Johnny boy," my dad said, the only one who got away with nicknames for our son. John wasn't a fan of being called any *cutesy names.* He liked being referred to by his proper name and nothing else, but for some reason, he didn't bother arguing with Grandpa about it.

"You were amazing, *Mijo*," Carmen said, leaning down and planting a big fat kiss on John's cheeks, leaving behind her ruby red lip marks on his face as he giggled. "Look at you, and *you*," she widened her eyes at Ruby Mackey. "This looks like young love, eh?"

I watched John's face turn ten shades of beet red while my dad laughed. Dad looked back at me, naturally amused by his gregarious wife, and then leaned down to pick up Kaley to make up for the two days he hadn't seen his granddaughter.

"It's not love," John immediately corrected Carmen, staring darkly at me as if I were the one who'd mortified him in front of the girl.

"Bye, John," Ruby said, taking her embarrassment over to the other side of the theater stage.

"Oh, *Mijo*. She is quite taken with your handsome looks," Carmen pressed on. "And I must say I don't blame her," she chuckled and winked back at me.

"Thanks, Grandma Carmen," John said, forcing himself to smile at her.

There was something about Carmen that allowed us all to be

extremely forgiving and amused by her when she did this type of shit to embarrass us in public. John was a perfect example of that now. Instead of getting pissed at her, his fiery gaze was on my ass as if I'd planned the whole thing. This was all very typical, though. It's how things were when my dad and Carmen were around the kids. Carmen danced around like a Mexican Fairy Godmother, entertaining all of us with her charm and boisterous personality, and we just rolled with it.

"So, are we ready to get dinner?" my dad asked. "My treat."

"Sure," I smiled. "John, grab your things, and we'll go."

"Where's Dad?" John asked, finally taking notice that Jake had missed another event.

"He got stuck in traffic," I said, feeling irritated by my husband's absence but ultimately used to it.

"Yeah, okay," John said, deflated. "Grandma Carm," John turned his attention to his favorite lady, "do you want to share a cinnamon roll with me?"

"Aw," Carmen smiled and ran her long red fingernails through John's hair, "you *know* I want to. Go grab your things, and you can ride with me and Papa to the diner."

"I'll be right back," John said with excitement.

"Where is Jacob?" my dad questioned after setting Kaley down so she could go get the doll she left in her chair. "He's missing out on all the good stuff. He's never going to get these moments back."

"I know, Dad," I answered with irritation. "Last I checked, I married a surgical chief and signed up for this way of life while raising kids. Don't start."

I hated defending Jake when he wasn't around for events like this because it was bullshit, especially since he planned on being here tonight. It was a complete letdown, but I was just thankful I had Carmen's jubilant energy, and my kids loved her like she was Mickey Mouse. I did, too. There were many times when being disappointed or let down by Jake made me sad, but fortunately, I had a great dad and a lively stepmom who kept all the sadness away when I felt it— kind of like right now.

"Well, they're only this age once, kid," Dad told me.

"Don't we all know it," I answered as if I were the one in trouble for Jake missing this whole thing because he was stuck in traffic. I wanted to kick Jake's ass after I read his text, but after he sent a video of a life flight chopper landing on the freeway, I knew there was nothing he could do but sit there and wait for ambulances, tow trucks, and California Highway Patrol to arrive and clear the thing. He was screwed, and I knew he was as upset about missing tonight as I was.

"All right, let's go," Dad said. He scooped up Kaley, grabbed John's hand, and ran to the exit like he was kidnapping them, making them laugh the whole way.

I was so thankful for these two people because they stepped in at every opportunity, not just helping Jake and me when we needed some alone time but also putting huge smiles on the kids' faces. And on nights like these, we needed that.

I WALKED INTO THE HOUSE, surprised to see the motion-activated lights turn on as if we were the first ones home.

"Where's Dad?" John questioned.

"I was about to ask the same thing," I answered him. "Go put your stuff upstairs in your room, and I'll call him."

"Cool," John said as Kaley started whining after waking up from dozing off in the car on the ride home.

"Let's get you to bed first," I said, picking her up and heading up the stairs to get her tucked in.

I walked past John's room and grinned while he put everything away in perfect order. "Did you want to call Dad and give him a hard time, or should I?" I teased.

"You can," John said, not too concerned with Jake's whereabouts. "I have to finish homework."

"You did so well tonight," I told him. "I sent your dad all the videos I took, so even though he wasn't there tonight, he sort of was."

"I know," John said. "It's cool, Mom."

This was just our everyday family life. There were plenty of times I eyed other parents, husbands and wives sitting in the crowd, and wished I had the cute little nine-to-five family, too, but I didn't. Truthfully, I wouldn't trade my husband or his love for the three of us for anything in the world. This was the life of being married to the big cardiovascular chief. We got him when he was off work, and nothing stood in the way of us then.

I could feel sorry for myself, but I wouldn't. I also wouldn't put any guilt on Jake because his job was his passion, and he was a brilliantly gifted surgeon who saved lives under impossible circumstances after other physicians had given up. Regardless, more and more these days, it felt like his job was who he was married to and more his family than we were. Nights like tonight sucked, and that was why I was willing to join forces with the other wives to get our workaholic husbands to plan for the holidays. Having them more involved, like we did on Halloween, worked out nicely, and the kids were thrilled to have their dads be a part of the holiday. It was lovely.

Seeing the disappointment in John's eyes tonight just reinforced my resolve to get Jake more involved. I knew that roping him into planning and attending a couple of holidays was not a permanent solution to our problem, but I needed to take action to bring back the spark that was starting to fizzle out in our marriage.

# CHAPTER 9

Ash

I finished custom wrapping one of my most expensive art pieces for a client who'd placed an online order and handed it to their assistant, who was sent to pick it up.

"Tell them I hope they enjoy it. If it doesn't meet with their expectations for their space, I will issue a full refund as promised," I told the young woman.

She smiled at me. "Mr. Hawk will most likely love this," Candace responded. "Mrs. Monroe wasn't lying when she said you were the artist to furnish multi-million-dollar beach homes."

The chime at my door announced the devil herself, Natalia Monroe. She pulled off her oversized, glam sunglasses as she floated into the gallery and smiled at the lovely young woman at my counter.

"Candace, I was hoping to catch you before Ash wrapped the damn thing," Nat acknowledged her with a hint of annoyance. "If there's one thing I can't stand, it's when I try to get my ass where I said I'd be on time, and fucking traffic ruins it all."

It was easy to see that Nat had some form of a relationship with Titus's assistant, which seemed natural since the Hawk brothers had entered a business relationship with Jim Mitchell and his VP, Nat's husband, Spencer. Nat handled the majority of their real estate transactions, and they all attended events and dinners together, so they were probably friends by now. And, to all of us, Candace seemed to be more than *just an assistant* to Titus Hawk.

"It's no big deal. Ashley is a talented artist, and Titus will be blown away with this piece," she looked back at me. "After he saw it online, he had to have it. I have to say it's even more beautiful in person. It looks almost three-dimensional; I can't imagine how you pulled that off."

I grinned. "I paint the entire canvas black and then gradually bring dark to light colors in. Somehow, that's the trick to creating that feature with my portraits."

"Well, I'm sure we will be back for more once Mr. Hawk sees this in person," she finished. "My driver is here, so I'm going to head out."

"Have a good day," I said.

"Tell Mr. Hawk I will see him tomorrow night at the Crown Gala," Nat said.

"Sure thing," she said, and then she disappeared out of the door.

"Let me lock this," I said. Candace came to pick up that portrait thirty minutes after I usually closed up shop, and I was eager to finish the day.

"That poor girl," Nat said with a sigh. "Blowing her boss while he's fucking every woman he meets at these events we all attend."

"Is Titus *that* bad?" I cringed.

Nat rolled her eyes. "You know the type all too well, Ashley. He's a typical gorgeous-as-hell young billionaire new to Los Angeles, and every woman wants him. He knows it, appreciates it, and enjoys it."

"Yeah," I said. "Does *she* know?"

"Of course not," Nat chuckled. "That's how men like Titus get away with this shit. I'd like to say it's willful ignorance, but you know how it goes. They make women feel like they're the one and only."

"I feel bad for her," I said.

"I don't," Nat said unsympathetically. "Any woman wrapping herself up in a man because she wants his money, or hell, even *love*, when he makes it obvious that he's not settling down anytime soon is asking for heartbreak."

"Yeah, but if he's playing her, she wouldn't know," I said. "She might think he could fall in love with her. Maybe that's what she hangs onto."

Nat folded her arms and smiled at me, "Your naivety is adorable."

I rolled my eyes, "There's nothing adorable about feeling bad for someone who is going to get their heart broken by a billionaire playboy."

"You think that girl doesn't know what she's working with?" Nat challenged.

"No, I honestly don't," I said. "I think it's pathetic that these men use their money and status to draw women in only to discard them when they get bored."

"Honey, don't get worked up about a tale that's old as time," Nat said in her usual sassy yet knowledgeable tone. "These women, *especially* Candace, know what they're signing up for with men like Titus and his brothers. Titus shows no shame by telling everyone he is staying on the market. Shit, she's most likely had to help a few of his *ladies* out of the house the next morning."

"Jesus, I can't imagine. Well, maybe she's not *blowing* him, like you suggested."

"She's definitely blowing him. I can spot a blower from a mile away and twenty thousand leagues under the sea," Nat confirmed, walking over to my sailboat portrait exhibits. "She wants more, but he won't let it get that far because she's already too attached. I see it all the time with these hot-lips assistants. The only thing these players won't do when they see that hopeful, fantasyland look in their eyes, like Candace has, is fuck them."

"Well, it's all the same if you ask me."

"Not for them," Nat said, knowing her way around the world of players. "Fucking and blowing are two very separate things. Blowing is just having a dick in your mouth, but fucking is more than that. It's seeing the look in his eyes when he slips his hard dick in you, knowing it's your glorious and wet vajayjay that's giving him pleasure, and when he can't hide his look of satisfaction and relief that you're giving him, that's when the emotional connection takes place. It's all wrapped up in the fact that he needs her for more than just sex, so once the sex happens, you have one happy assistant who's now staked a claim on a man who wants his freedom."

Just hearing Nat talk about seeing the pleasure in your man's eyes while he's climaxing was making me ache to be with Jake. I pictured that look on his face at the beginning of our relationship, and now that I thought about it, I hadn't seen that *look* since I'd been diagnosed with cancer and even after beating it. It grieved my heart to think that we were somehow drifting apart. Life had us both in its stronghold, and I didn't like it. I missed my goddamn husband.

"Ash? Honey, I didn't mean to upset you," Nat said. "You know how I get with this shit. Who knows, maybe Titus does have a thing for Candace. Only time will tell, but it's nothing for you to get upset about."

"It's not that," I said, wiping the tears from my eyes I hadn't felt streaming down my face. "I mean, I feel horrible for her, but you're right. I don't even know the man well, and people's choices are none of my business. We live and learn."

"Then what is it?" Nat questioned more seriously, moving on from the Candace and Titus gossip session we found ourselves in.

"I don't know. Maybe it's hormones. I've been in menopause since the surgery, and Dr. Aster told me this would be rough despite the hormone pills I'm taking."

"Is this about Jake? Have you dried up? Because not to worry, darling, there are a plethora of fabulous lubricants that Spence and I use when we—"

"No, no. No one is dried up yet," I chuckled. "And I don't need your sex therapy. All of God's creatures know that you and Spence have every sexual situation mastered."

"Well, I have some great lube brands if you need to help out Lady Ashley."

"Lady Ashley?" I said with a laugh. "I'm not a fucking duchess."

"You might not be a duchess, but your pussy is a queen that should not go unnoticed or become neglected."

"That's not my problem. *Lady Ashley* is performing well," I said.

"Well, then, what is it?"

"It's just that I feel like Jake and I are drifting apart from the responsibilities of life: his job, my job, and the kids. All of it."

"Oh, sweetheart, this is why I didn't allow Spencer to pick out his own costume for the Halloween event. I was getting dangerously close to feeling how you are feeling right now, and he was oblivious, so I turned that man's ass into Big Bird. Once he saw my and our daughter's admiration, he was instantly reminded that being married to me was more rewarding than work and landing billion-dollar deals."

"Jake's not like that, though, and I feel bad even talking about it."

"Don't feel bad at all. That's what we girls are here for. You're feeling lonely, and you miss your husband. Why would you feel shame for admitting that?"

"Because it's not really his fault. He tries his hardest to be there with all of us, but his job pulls him away. I don't want—" I couldn't even think. "I don't know. I feel selfish even talking about this. Jake's one of the best heart surgeons on the planet, so it's not like he's out fucking around. He's saving people's lives every day. I knew that when I met and fell in love with him. I knew what I was getting into when he proposed, and I said yes. I knew all of this."

"You might have known it," Nat said, "but you didn't *know this* feeling of loneliness in your marriage. Have you talked to Jake about this?"

"No," I said. "I would only feel like I was adding more to his already full plate."

"Okay," Nat smirked at me sympathetically, "you're not alone in how you're feeling."

"Really? You too?"

"Me? Oh, hell to the fuck no," she said, looking at me like I asked if she would consider becoming a nun. "Honey, when I feel lonely, my man *hears* about it. Spence already knows he's lucky to be married to my ass, just as Jake knows he's lucky to have you. Unfortunately, I'm seeing a very troubling trend amongst my lady friends. What is happening with you and Jake sounds like what I'm seeing and hearing from Collin and Elena."

"Elena hasn't said anything to me about feeling lonely with Collin these days. I hadn't noticed anything, either."

"That's because you're not as good at seeing the sadness in a lonely woman's eyes as I am. Think about it. Jake and Collin are both chief of their specialties at that damn hospital, and they never have time off. Fucking ever."

"I didn't even think about Laney."

"Well, I came up with a little plan for her and Mr. Brooks to revive that famous spark of theirs, and it's high time I share it with you, too, because Jim is about to give two of his surgeons time off around the holidays to be with their wives on a very sexy love fest vacation."

"Nat, we can't," I immediately stopped her. "Seriously. We have the kids, and they miss Jake as much as I do."

"The kids will be fine," Nat said. "The kids will be worse off if their parents drift apart and end up divorced. That shit can't happen. We need to take care of the intimacy that's lacking between Mom and Dad, and then, trust me when I tell you, the kids will be rewarded when you all get home just in time for Christmas."

"I don't know about this."

"That's why the spark is dead in your relationship, my love," Nat said with a laugh. "If you want to revive it, you've got to go back to the bold and daring ways from the beginning of you and Jake."

"In the beginning, we hooked up on a one-night stand."

"Ah, the thrill," Nat said, closing her eyes and inhaling deeply through her nose, no doubt imagining the many one-night stands she'd enjoyed. "Do you remember how it made you feel that night and then long afterward when you and Jake inevitably met again for the first time?"

Adrenaline coursed through my body at the reminder of when

Jake and I first met. How daring and exciting it was and how badly I wanted to feel all that again. I craved it and him more than I knew.

"That smile and look in your eyes is telling me the answer I need," she grinned. "Get your cute little ass home to those adorable kids, and let me and Spence talk with Jim. We'll handle the rest. You, Jake, Collin, and Elena will return home just in time for Christmas week, and you can celebrate with the rest of us with the renewed love that you sexy mommas desperately need. And, of course, Jake and Collin can kiss my ass later for saving their marriages."

"What is this big plan?"

"Sit tight while I pull up the resort and destination that I surprised Spence with a year ago. This is going to perk *Lady Ashley* right up, sweetheart."

# CHAPTER 10

❄

Jake

The past week at work went exceptionally well, and I was proud of myself for not bringing it home and dragging it through the front door to my family. My awesome ass even brought dinner home twice this week after I managed to get out of the office only one hour late instead of my usual three.

I was doing a fantastic job and making monumental efforts to make up for missing my son's band recital and then falling asleep on Ash while she told me about it.

"Monumental efforts, huh?" my brother's humored voice rang through my ears while I continued to chew on the steak I'd just taken a bite of.

"You heard me," I said. "After missing John's big night, I've had my family-man mode cranked up. I put more effort into getting out of the office early and bringing home dinner not once," I held up a finger and eyed him and the men at our secluded table with a cocky smile, "but twice."

"Here! Here!" Spencer, my brother's VP, said in a smart-ass tone. "To leaving work only *one* hour after closing time instead of three to five hours after that."

Collin smirked at me. "That's all fine and well, but you fell asleep on Ash while she was telling you about John's big night. Dipfucker move, man," he said.

I placed my steak knife and fork on each side of my plate and faced Collin's smile. I eyed my brother's best friend, Alex, who had a shit-eating grin, too, "That was supposed to be between me and you," I said to Collin. "But since we have the whole fucking gang sitting here with their self-righteous moods, they all know too."

"Hey, I'm just taking lessons on how not to fuck shit up again with Darcy," Sebastian Aster said.

I smiled at my screwed-in-love friend, "You know, when I first met you Asters, I thought you all were a bunch of fucked-up East Coast billionaire dicks."

Sebastian and his brother, John, grinned at each other, knowing I was correct in that assessment.

"You would be one hundred percent on that," John Aster confirmed. "However, we're not as stupid as we look, and now look at you. You *love* us."

"Careful with that. He's all mine, bitch," Collin teased.

"What's going on with you and Darcy anyway?" I decided to pry into Sebastian and Darcy's situation, getting the spotlight off me.

In the company of these CEOs and doctors, who survived on giving each other shit at these dinners a couple of times a month, you didn't want the target on your back.

"Darcy has agreed to move from Mexico," Sebastian said with a *just-fucked my girl* smile.

"No shit?" Jim said, sipping his bourbon. "What did you say to get her to jump finally?"

"Nothing. We've just been dating and taking it slow, and unlike Jakey here," he smirked at me, "I'm ensuring I give her more time than my job. It's helping the relationship flourish."

"The fuck?" I said with annoyance.

"And the troubled marriage case is back on the table," Alex said with a chuckle while Spencer smirked at him, making me wonder if they knew something I didn't.

"The troubled marriage case?" I said, looking at Collin for help. "Where the fuck is Brandt tonight, anyway? Last time we all sat around this damned round table, his ass was the one in trouble with the lady."

"Dipshit is proposing to Jessa," Collin said. "Finally took my advice and stopped fucking around. Well, not proposing, but getting the whole venue, ring, and pomp and circumstance together to make it happen."

"Well, it's easy to say he's doing better than us then," I answered.

"Speak for yourself," Jim said with the same grin I'd seen him, Sebastian, Spencer, and Alex trading back and forth with each other all fucking night. "My wife is extremely content with our marriage."

"What the hell is going on here?" I questioned, feeling an ambush coming on.

"We're eating dinner," Sebastian said.

"No," Collin finally stepped up after realizing something fishy was happening. "Jake's right. You're all making too much of an issue about Jake and Ash for the information he's given you."

"Thanks, man," I said, knowing Collin would always be my ride or die.

"No problem, lover," he teased.

"You're up the same fucking creek as your boyfriend," Spencer said with his usual arrogance.

"If you know something we don't, Monroe, you'd better spill it now," I said.

"You think everything's fine because you've called out for dinner twice this week, yet you're out with the guys tonight instead of with your beautiful wife?" Sebastian chimed in.

He knew something, too. I swear this was like high school life all over again, except Jim's best buds were all executives who ran companies. Mine were doctors who, since we were all keeping score tonight, were a bunch of screw-ups barely hanging onto their marriages. Except for John Aster, I guess. He and Mickie were inseparable, but they shared the same profession and worked in the same office, so they didn't count.

"No, Jake's onto something," Collin said, waving his fork toward the four smirking men across from us. "You dipfucks know something we don't. Better start talking," Collin challenged.

"It's nothing. It's just that word got to Avery that Ash is having a tough time right now, being lonely and shit," Jim diffused the escalating conversation.

Collin chuckled. "Never a good idea to let the wife become lonely, man," he said while I glared at him.

I felt hurt that Ash felt this way so much that she'd brought it to Avery's attention, and now, it was coming up at the dinner table with the men. Fuck me. Seb was right; I shouldn't be here. I should be at home with her and the kids on a Friday night.

"Your ass is in the same boat as Jake's, Col," Alex said. "Seems you both have lonely wives at home, raising kids while that hospital takes up all your free time."

I frowned, "If it were that bad, Ash would've definitely told me."

"But she didn't, did she?" Spencer said. "She told Nat, though. And once *my wife* gets involved, you know it's all coming out, and one of us or all of us is going to pay."

"Speak for yourself, Big Bird," Collin said, making fun of the Halloween costume his wife had made him wear.

"Wait," I said. "Nat knows my wife is lonely?"

"Better Nat than the fucking pool boy," Alex said.

"Listen, it's not all bad. Because of this, you two dumbasses are getting time off for a romantic little getaway," Jim said.

"What are you talking about? I can't just take time off work and leave the hospital and my patients for a romantic getaway," I looked at Collin to see if I was the only one who hadn't lost their mind at the table.

"Can you afford a divorce?" Alex said.

"No, and don't be ridiculous. That isn't going to happen. I'm going to go home, talk to my wife, and we're going to clear this shit up."

"Sit down," Jim said with a sigh. "No, it's not all that bad. But yes, I've talked to Dr. Stone, and he will assume your responsibilities while you're away with Ash. And you," he looked at Collin. "Your main man, Dr. Mutton, will cover for you."

"I'm completely lost," Collin said. "Laney hasn't mentioned shit about shit to me."

"You're never home, dipshit," Spencer said. "Listen, Nat suggested that Jim give you two overworked doctors some time away just before the holidays to go on this sex retreat that Nat and I just got back from."

"Fucking hell," Sebastian laughed. "It seems neither doctor is arguing, and from the looks on their faces, they're more than happy to hand over the reins for a much-needed break."

"No shit," I said. "When I think about it, I haven't had a *real* vacation since my honeymoon. It's always meeting up somewhere and taking the jet back early for work."

"Exactly," Jim smiled. "You'll both thank me and Spence later for giving you the time off."

"What's the fucking catch?" Collin asked, slow to take the bait.

"Smart man," I said, looking at my best friend. "This is all too fairytale easy, make your wife's dreams come true type shit."

"There is no catch unless you don't like sex," Spencer said with a grin I didn't trust.

"How can we trust you both aren't sending us to the fucking desert or something? There's always a catch with you assholes," I said.

"No catch. You'll be taking the private jet to the Maldives for this exclusive retreat," Jim said.

"Why us?" Collin said.

"It's not for you," Spencer advised. "It's for your wives and families." Spencer studied the looks of speculation on my and Collin's faces. "Listen, just because you two dipshits are all about pranking us over the holidays doesn't mean we're doing the same with you guys."

I twisted my lips in thought while I leaned back and crossed my arms. "Something doesn't seem *promising* about this," I said.

"Well, we do go hard on all their asses during the holidays. I'd imagine they'd beg for an excuse to kick us out of here to save themselves," Collin said, shrugging.

"And it is a sex retreat that the two biggest sex freaks of all of us went to," I said to Collin. "Fine, we're down, but I want to speak to each of my patients first and see if they'll be fine with Stone or prefer to wait for my return."

"When are we going to this?" Collin asked, both of us feeling very singled out.

"You leave the day after Thanksgiving and return the week before Christmas," Jim said.

"Shit," I said. "That's a week from today."

"So, you better get packed," Spencer smirked, and when he, Sebastian, and my brother exchanged *too* gleeful of a smile, I narrowed my eyes.

Ah, fuck it. I was only worried because Collin and I had played some funky pranks on all these guys, but they weren't like us and definitely wouldn't do anything to upset Ash or Laney.

My sinking feeling was that Ash felt lonely, and I had no clue. Of course, there had been signs of her loneliness, and work kept us apart a lot these days; I just didn't understand why she didn't come to me with it.

Oh, right...perhaps it was all the times I fell asleep while she talked to me about her day. Fuck, I could kick my own ass for all this, but I was thankful that my brother and Spencer had ensured the hospital would give us the time off we needed to share it with our wives. It didn't need to be some weird sex getaway, but what the hell. Nat and Spence were known for some wild shit, and I was curious about where those two played around when Nat whisked him off and around the globe to *rekindle* their flame every other fucking month.

I didn't like the reason that Ash and I were taking this trip alongside Collin and Elena, but I was happy to do it. All that one-on-one time and time spent with our closest friends was bound to draw us closer together again.

# CHAPTER 11

❄

Jake

W e were on the eve of our retreat, and my excited ass was trying to keep it no more than twenty miles per hour over the speed limit while driving the kids to Ash's dad and Carmen's place. The more I thought about checking back into the beginning of my relationship with Ash, the more excited I became.

Even without this escape, which I was fortunate enough to have been given, I'd already snapped my busy ass back into place, being more present with the kids and my wife. Even Collin jumped at the chance to bring things back to how they were in the early days of his and Elena's relationship. He'd even gone so far as to recreate the moment when he'd purchased their first Christmas tree, which was dead and brown thanks to my pranks, so it was safe to say this retreat would be taking lessons from me and my best friend instead of the other way around.

We'd figured out exactly what to do, all without having to go to some *intimacy spa & retreat* to keep the spark alive in our relationships. That's how Collin and I rolled. Nothing ever beat us.

It was cool that Collin and Elena were on the same *journey* of rediscovering their intimacy as Ash and I were; however, because of the seclusion of the villas, which were built over water, and the fact that we were doing this to give our wives the attention they were craving, I suspected we'd hardly see each other.

I could hardly wait for tomorrow morning. The wheels of the Mitchell and Associates private jet couldn't land at our destination fast enough for my liking.

"So, you and Ash must revive the forgotten love?" Carmen said, tasting the enchilada sauce that she was making for our kids' favorite dish.

"Meh," I shrugged. Ash and I weren't in *that* much of a bad place in our marriage. "We're not reviving anything, Carm," I said, taking a sip of the beer she offered me when I first arrived with the kids. "We're just using this trip to enhance what we already have going."

Carmen smiled at me with the same look I'd seen on everyone else's faces when discussing this getaway. It was half the reason Collin and I stepped up the game with our wives and ensured we carried more of the load with the kids to ease that burden for them, too. It felt like everyone knew something we didn't.

"What's that look?" I finally called her out.

"Look? There is no look, *Mijo*," she said, pursing her lips in humor and pinching my cheek as if I were a little boy. "I just can't wait to hear all about this when you lovebirds return renewed, refreshed, and restored."

"I looked this place up," I eyed her mysterious grin with speculation, "and you should know that my lady will be one fulfilled woman when we get home."

She chuckled. "Oh, I know," she arched a knowing eyebrow at me. "When Ash told me about the retreat and spa you four were attending, and I saw that it was practically the mothership calling Ashley home, I couldn't have been more thrilled for you."

"That's the thing," I said, concerned *again* about this trip even though I swear I looked it up. It seemed to be the ultimate paradise, so I didn't understand what everyone was going on about. "You all seem like you know something I don't know."

"Does this bother you?" she playfully said.

"Immensely," I answered.

"Good," she nodded. "Sometimes it's nice to be humbled in ways we don't expect."

I frowned. I wouldn't get anywhere with Carmen on this, and I definitely wouldn't with Ash's dad. It felt like somehow Collin and I were busted, but for what? Jesus, we were two fucking doctors who didn't work nine-to-five jobs. Ash and Laney understood that, and in the past couple of weeks, we'd been putting forth a lot more effort.

So why did this all feel like it was a setup?

*Ring! Ring!*

"Collin, hang on a sec," I answered my phone. "I've gotta take this, Carm," I leaned toward Carm, kissing her on the cheek. "Have fun with the kids. I've hired a company to have the beach house fully decorated for Christmas once we get home."

"You've thought of it all," she patted my cheek. "Go enjoy your beautiful wife. We have some exciting plans for the kids. I promise they won't miss you while you're gone."

"They never do when they're with you guys," I chuckled. "Tell Mark I'm sorry I missed him."

"I will," she smiled, then her phone rang to interrupt our farewells. She gave me a kiss on the cheek, and I headed out.

"Sorry, dude. You there?" I said, getting in Ash's Range Rover and allowing the Bluetooth to pick up the call with Collin.

"Yeah, and if you always keep Ash waiting like you just did me, I understand why you're joining me on this love renewal trip."

I could hear the agitation in Collin's voice, and it wasn't because I made him wait. I had an inkling he felt the same way I did.

"What's your problem? You should be as excited as I am to get out of here for a while."

"That's the thing," Collin said. "You just dropped the kids off at Ash's parents, right?"

"Yep," I said, pulling out of the neighborhood and down the street that would lead me to the freeway. "I was saying goodbye to Carm—"

"I just dropped our kids off, too," Collin said.

"Okay?"

"And Miguel seems way too fucking excited to know we're going on this little *sex trip* with our wives," he said.

I narrowed my eyes. "Carmen was the same way," I answered. "I don't want to think there's more to this, but shit, man. From the way we're forever fucking with everyone, I think they just want to see us sweat. Seriously, what the fuck can go wrong?"

"True. We are going to the Maldives," he answered.

"And yes, I *was* concerned after Jim and Avery acted weird about it, too. I was starting to believe that the fucking jet was going to leave us in Dubai during the layover or some shit, but—"

"Yeah, Laney is packed with swimsuits and clothes for the tropics. I thought the same thing about ditching us, but I was leaning more toward them landing our asses in Iceland or some shit."

"You know they'd love to see our faces when we got back, and they asked if Santa Claus was at the North Pole, coaching us on how to love and appreciate our wives like he does Mrs. Claus," I said.

"Well, fuck. What if that's what's going on? This could all be one big ass prank to get us back. I could see your little son heading that up since you pranked him about Santa not coming last year."

My lips twisted. John had a vengeful streak when the mood struck, and if his uncles were all asking for ideas, my son would spearhead the project.

"Nah. Although highly believable," I answered Collin. "John knew exactly why Santa put a lump of coal under the tree. After he took back his threat of telling his sister that Santa wasn't real, we showed him where the gifts were hidden. So, the Santa beef should be squashed."

"You think we're just being paranoid?"

"We're not paranoid. We're just not gullible and stupid," I said.

"So, what are we going to do?"

"Well, if these jokesters dare to fuck with us, we'll spend the entire trip planning and plotting how to get them back. Jim's not that dumb. He grew up with me and knows I won't just roll over. I'll dish it right back."

"Then why does something feel off?" Collin asked.

"If we don't board the same jet as our lovely wives, we'll know something is up. If we do? Then we're good."

"I'm packing warm clothes just in case," Collin said. "I don't trust these fools."

"Well, firstly, we're flying private, so we can pack our entire wardrobe. Secondly, the guys would fuck with you and me, not our wives. You know that."

"So, you think we're really getting two solid weeks of alone time with Ash and Laney?"

"Let's hope so," I said.

"Okay. No more overthinking," Collin agreed hesitantly.

"Well, wheels are up on that jet at seven in the morning. So, finish packing, and if this is a prank, let's make the most out of it for the ladies."

With that all discussed and out of the way, I relaxed. If this were a prank, it would amuse the hell out of Ash and Laney, and that's how Collin and I operated anyway. We loved making everyone laugh, even if it was at our own expense.

It had been way too fucking long since I'd had quality alone time with Ash. So, all that mattered was that I was with her. I didn't care where we were so long as we were together.

# CHAPTER 12

❄

Ash

Thank God Jim owned the private jet company that housed dozens of charter jets, turning what would've been a two-day flight into one. I wasn't one to cash in on all the luxuries that being married to a billionaire offered, but when it came to traveling, I was more than willing to take advantage.

"Okay, so," Jake said, grinning from ear to ear, "where's our sex shack, baby?"

I looked over at Elena, knowing this would be the hardest part of this trip. In fact, I was dreading it, but I was going with the flow. The holistic and wellness approach for all of us to detox the stress of our lives would improve this experience. It was part of the wellness and intimacy therapy retreat, and it had been far too long since I'd grounded my energy. Jake was never really into this type of thing, but I knew he would love it.

After this first part was over, of course.

"That look?" Jake frowned, studying my face as we stood in the entryway of the retreat. "What the hell is *that* look?"

"Ladies and Gentlemen, husbands and wives," a man announced, wearing a vibrant, multi-colored scarf around his waist—wearing *only* that.

Jake and Collin snapped around, and their eyes widened like they'd just witnessed a murder.

"Careful, my man. One gust of wind and your fancy scarf will be long gone. Then I'm *really* going to need sex therapy," Collin said, prompting the man to smirk as if he couldn't wait to get the sessions started.

"You will be wearing one as well," the man said. "I am Gustoff Lauyanance," he started, speaking to all the couples waiting for instructions on where to put our luggage.

"If I'm wearing nothing but that scarf, angel," Jake eyed me with a flirty look that I hadn't seen on his face in forever, "you're not going to be able to get me off of—"

"If I may have order and silence, please," the man interrupted Jake screwing around. "Ladies," he held out his hand toward where staff waited with silk cloths folded neatly in their arms, "please join Hammond and her team. You will be taken and instructed for your coaching sessions, which will begin as soon as you are changed."

"I'll see you tonight," I said with a smile to Jake. I kissed his cheek and prayed the man would cooperate and follow his yoga and meditation instructors.

"Yes, yes," Gustoff said with a bright smile. "I nearly forgot. Please kiss and say your farewells to your spouses and partners," he offered with a nod. "Once everyone is detoxed, cleansed, and, of course, educated, you will rejoin your loved one and begin practicing your newly enlightened and awakened routine of love and passion."

"What the hell?" Jake and Collin said in unison while I thought it in my head.

"Gustoff," Collin started before Jake could, "I do hope your cute little session lasts no longer than a couple of hours because I've got plans to *practice* my enlightened, passionate moves on my wife."

"This, friends, is why the detoxification process usually takes longer with the male subjects," Gustoff stated. "Ego death is very hard to achieve with our masculine friends. Though not impossible, it does take time."

"Ego death?" Jake said, looking at me as if I knew what that meant. "What the fuck is he talking about?"

"You will learn," Gustoff said to Collin and Jake, who seemed to be the only males in the room who couldn't remain silent long enough for us to get our instructions. "You will also learn that using curse words to frame a question for your partner is forbidden here on the island."

"Forbidden? Where the hell are we even at?" Collin said, looking at Jake, then back to Gustoff. "I *framed* that question for my best buddy here, not my wife. So, look at me; ego death is already happening."

Unsurprisingly, Gustoff seemed to be losing his patience with the two men. Laney and I could only cover our mouths to hide our smiles at what Spencer, Jim, Sebastian, and Alex had arranged. Sure, they had sent us on a love retreat, but for Jake and Collin, it was like trying to get two hyper kindergartners to meditate. I wouldn't be surprised if Jim had cameras everywhere to watch the guys' meltdown in real time.

Honestly, I was a total yogi who tried to meditate every day, but even this seemed like it might be an extreme version of what I thought was normal. And what I thought was normal was equivalent to being a full-blown hippie to everyone else I knew, so I couldn't imagine how this was going to go for the guys.

"It's easy to see you are not fully aware of how our intimacy sessions work here," Gustoff said.

"All I saw was the hut I would be staying in with my wife," Jake said.

"We refer to those as our overwater bungalows," Gustoff corrected Jake. "Your wives will be staying there while going through their meditations and personal masturbations."

"*Excuse* me, what?" Collin said. "What is happening?"

"I truly hope we can achieve ego death with you both," Gustoff said, eyeing them skeptically. "If not, you will not rejoin your wives in your designated bungalows."

"Understood," Jake grimly answered. "How long, *sir*, does it take for, let's say," he pointed at a man in a business suit, staring at him with irritation, "a *normal* guy like him, who doesn't curse or even speak up, to achieve ego death?"

"Five to seven days," Gustoff answered, prompting Jake and Collin to shut their mouths and follow Gustoff's lead. "For you and your friend, I'm concerned. It's not impossible, but much detoxification must be done."

"Jesus God. They're turning us into monks for a fucking week? I *will* murder my brother when we get home," Jake said to Collin.

"You have much to heal, young man. You speak of murder and frame it as a joke, mocking spiritual people. You have no shame."

Jake's jaw clenched tightly, and it took all my strength not to burst out laughing. I felt Jake's pain because this seemed ridiculous, especially for a nonbeliever who thought he had nothing to gain. I knew those boys well enough to know it was taking every thread of energy they possessed not to unleash on Gustoff.

"I gotta be honest here, Gus," Jake said. "I'm just a little pissed the fuck off at this very moment. I thought this was a sex retreat, not a goddamn *situation* where I'm being judged for saying things my drug-addict mother taught me."

"That is interesting. We will discuss the culprit for your anger issues in one of your therapy sessions tomorrow," Gustoff said. "Ladies, join Hammond, would you please? Gentlemen, follow me."

That's all that was said before Jake and Collin were led away with the other men. Jake didn't even look back at me to say goodbye, which was a relief because I wouldn't have been able to hold in my laughter if he had.

"I can't even imagine the shit Jake and Collin will give that group," Laney said with a laugh.

"You know I'm all about this stuff, but I think we're at extreme levels here," I whispered.

"No shit. That's why I wish I could be a fly on the wall with whatever the men will be going through."

"I have a feeling Jim had to have set this all up to be like this?"

"I wouldn't doubt it," Laney said. "I imagine everyone who had a hand in sending us here helped create this environment."

"Well, hopefully, we'll smash through this ego death thing quick and be lounging in our bungalows when the men return, detoxed and refreshed."

"Knowing Jake and Collin, they'll probably just sneak over to us at night for a quickie without getting caught," Laney said a little too loudly.

"The men are being shuttled further inland. They will be miles away from the bungalows," Hammond said in a soft and soothing voice. "There is no way they will be able to escape the destination where they are being taken."

I laughed out loud. "My husband will find a way, especially since you just used the word *escape*," I said in complete disbelief at where we'd all ended up. "We shall see."

"That we shall," Hammond said with a smile. "Now, allow me to bring all of you into our first session room, where we have raw vegetables and fish to eat to begin your detoxification process."

If this didn't bring Jake and me closer together intimacy-wise, it would surely expedite the divorce process.

# CHAPTER 13

❄

Jake

Collin and I had no other option at this point but to shut our fucking mouths. I had no idea what to think, say, or do anyway, so watching the ocean—which we flew twenty fucking hours to get to —disappear in the distance was about all I could do.

I would've loved to call my brother or one of the bastards who were behind this and lay waste to their asses; unfortunately, part of this fuckery was to confiscate our cell phones before we loaded up in this caravan of pathetic husbands who spent way too much money to find the spark in their marriages again.

"So, you're facing divorce, too, eh?" the man sitting in front of me in this godforsaken, rickety bus asked.

Our transportation seemed scarily like a prison transport, minus the chains…for now.

I glanced over at Collin, who sat across the aisle from me and saw him smirk at the man. The dude was a good-looking, put-together individual, but in a few minutes, he'd be stripped out of his business suit and wearing the same mother fucking tunic I'd be forced to wear.

"What makes you think I'm facing divorce?" I questioned his probe into my personal life.

"Why else would you pay eighty thousand dollars to restore your marriage?"

I had no idea what my expression was in response to this man, but it made him glance over at Collin and then back to me to see if I'd pulled it together.

"You paid eighty thousand dollars to *restore* your marriage?" Collin asked with a humorous tone in his voice, leaving my mind to reel in shock at what I'd just heard.

"Yeah," the man answered. "Eighty thousand for me and eighty thousand for my wife."

"God in heaven," I said with equal parts disbelief and disgust. "Why on earth would you pay that kind of money for some bizarre vacation like this?"

"Because I've tried everything. She doesn't love me anymore. I lost my way in our marriage and neglected her. I tried taking her on numerous vacations to get her to fall in love with me again, but nothing has worked."

"Hold up," I said before pausing, trying to gather my thoughts because I was wildly confused. "So, this is the last-ditch effort? Maybe your wife just doesn't love you anymore, and maybe the marriage is over. That isn't only *your* fault."

"Keep your voice down," Collin said, glancing to the front of this Freddy Krueger bus. "Gustoff just looked back here."

"Listen," I whispered to the man, who was clearly heartbroken. "You're a good-looking dude, and from the amount of money you've thrown down on this place, it's fair to say that you're doing well in life financially. I'm sorry you can't get your wife into bed with you, or whatever, but the most important question here is this: do *you* feel responsible for your marriage being where it's at right now?"

"I do. I neglected her," he answered.

"Fair enough," I answered, shrugging my shoulders. "It seems my ass is planted on the seat behind you because my wife is feeling the same as yours. But shit, man, it takes two to make it and two to break it."

"He's right," Collin agreed, having my back since we were all in the same boat. "My guess is you're not the only one responsible."

"Well, she's made it clear that she's done fighting for what we used to have, and I didn't believe her until she left me. We've been living apart for a few months. This is all my fault," he practically moaned while wiping tears from his eyes.

*How the fuck did I wind up in this situation?*

"Perhaps Gus will help you achieve that ego death, and then all will be right in your world again," I said, entirely out of my depth in this conversation. "It seems like you are the one who forked over a hundred and sixty thousand dollars to sit on this bus with me and my buddy here. At least you're trying."

Collin spoke up and said, "I would understand if you're taking the blame because you've been cheating on your wife or something, but if you're here solely because she fell out of love with you, then I have to agree with Jakey," he pointed at me. "It's not all on you, my man."

"Well, that's how I feel," the guy answered.

My mood had been on a steady decline since we arrived at this retreat, and homeboy in front of me was only making things worse. I was no longer in the mood to speak to this fucker or even feel the energy of his fucked-up situation.

I sighed, closed my eyes, and pinched the bridge of my nose, hoping that maybe this was just a twisted dream. That would've at least made sense as to why I was being taken to some unknown place on this island to kill my ego and get therapy for my childhood trauma.

"We have reached the master house. We now request that no one speak until they've arrived at their rooms, changed, and meet back in the great hall for further instructions," Gustoff said when the bus came to a stop. He clasped his hands together, smiled warmly at all of us, and nodded, "I trust that all of you are here to learn the depths of being in one union with your spouse and going back to the days when you felt the desire and primal urge to spend the rest of your lives together. These things are so easily forgotten while embarking on the tiresome and difficult paths we travel. However, you will quickly learn that there is more to life than the wealth in your bank accounts."

I narrowed my eyes at the man. "Hey, Gustoff?" I questioned, raising my hand more to mock him than anything.

"You again," he responded as if I were *his* nightmare instead of the other way around. "What is it you need?"

"I'm just curious," I continued. "It sounds like you're saying that we all think money is the only thing for us in life?"

"Indeed. Money and the drive to find happiness through that method of energy are the main reasons marriages waste away."

"I've heard that, yes," I decided to agree with him not to be a complete dick.

"It is good to see you already understand the beginning of the truths that shall set—"

"I just don't understand why you're up there preaching how money is the reason we're losing our marriages while your cute little prison camp takes a substantial amount of that in order to train us not to depend on it for our well-being and happiness?"

"Excellent point," Collin agreed in my assessment that this was all a big scam.

"You will learn to appreciate the reason you paid the high price of this program. When you learn that, and after sacrificing time alone with your wives, you will also understand that it was not money that ruined or saved your marriage. Money is energy. You must expel that energy from your minds and lives to achieve the proper..."

The man's voice drifted into the background of my mind, and I glanced over at Collin, wondering how the *fuck* he and I were going to survive this shit. I didn't speak *or think* in this manner at all. I was a fucking surgeon, for shit's sake, a scientist. Everything in my world was black and white and tangible. If my wife had a smile on her face after I took her to dinner, that meant she was happy. If my wife was pissed that I missed John's band recital, she wore *that* look on her face, too.

Suddenly, I was supposed to comprehend stupid shit like money being energy? Money paid the bills. Money put food on the damn table. Money was the only fucking way people could survive in any economy. I was lucky to have more of it than ninety-nine percent of the population, but I wasn't *in love* with it. If that's what this dumb hippie fucker was insinuating, he was wrong.

What the fuck was I doing here? I was going to chalk this up as the *one* prank my brother had ever pulled off, and I would take immense joy in paying him back for it.

# CHAPTER 14

Jake

"You awake?" I heard Collin whisper from the bunk above mine. I had almost drifted off to sleep, and now this.

"No," I tried to keep my mind from rousing too much. The more I slept, the quicker this would be over.

The next thing I knew, Collin's head was hanging over his bed, and the moonlight that shone through the thatched walls of our jungle hut gave me the perfect silhouette of my best friend's restless face.

"What the fuck are we going to do?"

"Sleep. Kill our egos. Get back to our wives," I said, closing my eyes.

"You realize the shit they gave us to eat tonight is supposed to cleanse our bowels, right?"

"That's what all detox places say at these little spiritual movements. Trust me, papaya and senna leaf teas are just hype. We'll be fine."

"We're fucked, man," he said.

"We're going to be fucked if we can't fake it to make it in this hellish situation."

"No. You know Kimberly, my RN? You've met her, right?"

"You mean the one who tried to seduce your married ass?" I asked. "Didn't she get fired over that?"

"Yeah, but before she mistook my kindness for interest, she confided in me about this particular detox process she went through. She told me that she shitted her brains out for twenty-four hours straight after drinking that tea."

"Damn. You two *did* get close if you had a woman confide in you about her poop," I answered. "No wonder you're on this joyride to hell with me."

"Never mind that," Collin said. "When that dude named Kavah made us drink that tea and he used the word senna, it reminded me of her and the stuff she took. Although the stuff she took was called *Smooth Move.*"

"Well, it's a wonder you got out of the grievance she filed against you when you backed out of the relationship that she said *you* led her on with. She was *obviously* baring her soul to you. You're such a tease."

"I'm being fucking serious, dude," he said.

"So am I," I answered. "And I'm trying to go to sleep so I don't go ape shit tomorrow when they feed us blended grass for breakfast."

"While you were in conversation with that poor bastard whose marriage is *actually* in legit trouble," he continued, ignoring me, "I was paying attention to the road we were taking to get here. We could get back to where our wives are, get kicked the fuck out of this place, and be home in two days to beat everyone's ass who planned this prank."

"Two days?"

"That's including the flight."

"Knowing my brother and the rest of those assholes, they already know we will come up with some stupid plan like that. Jim won't let the jet leave until we've done our time, man. We're fucked."

"It'll take us three hours on foot to get back to the girls," he said. "I'm *not* doing this shit. I don't need to detox. I don't need fucking therapy, and I sure as hell don't need a week away from my wife."

"A week *only* if you achieve *ego death*," I reminded him. "I'm telling you, we have to fake it and act like we're into whatever Mother Earth and the Universe wants for us to change our lives and thinking processes."

"Fuck," he seethed. "I just thought of something."

"I thought you'd thought of everything already," I said with a soft laugh.

"What if they're giving us the shits so we don't sneak out of here to get back to Laney and Ash?"

"I think that's the game plan," I answered as my stomach made a noise that sounded like a boar dying.

"What the hell?" Collin said as I became suddenly nauseated and sweaty. "Oh, no. Your detox process is already starting."

"Where's the fucking toilet?" I damn neared yelled, not sure if shit was oozing out of my tightened and very resistant asshole.

"We have to go outside, remember? Dig our own holes like hunters while the wives gather or whatever?"

I didn't have time to get angry, think, or even fucking respond to this curse of the shits that'd been cast over me. The gut-wrenching pain in my belly grew as I nearly shit all over myself whilst storming down the wooden steps of our makeshift hut. My guts were begging to be relieved as I dug my hands like claws into the dirt, opening a shallow hole that I wasn't sure would be deep enough for the lava that was about to flow explosively from my terrified butthole.

I didn't care how deep it was. Whatever was plugging the explosiveness was about to peek out of my ass like a turtle coming out of his shell, so I spun around, dropped my drawers, and let her rip. Luckily, I was more innovative than the average bear and knew how to be resourceful. So, while I shit, I dug another hole in front of me, working that mother fucker deep and wide like a World War Two foxhole. With the way my stomach was making noises and the cramps that were something that made me think of Ash in labor with our children, I knew I had to prepare myself to make whatever peace I could with my creator as my bowels released the toxins I was told I had in them.

"I'm never eating fast food again," a pathetic mutter came from a man about six feet away.

"Oh, what the fuck?" I said, no longer feeling like I was in a private and peaceful setting in this dense forest filled with ferns and banana trees. I would probably be so damn traumatized after this that I'd never visit a tropical island again.

"Yeah, they said that the—"

"Why are you out here?" I questioned, shocked I had no privacy in this asinine situation I never imagined myself to be in.

"It's the only place to shit, man," he said.

I half smiled. "Well, if I start calling on angels to take me, I'm sure you'll understand," I said when another sharp cramp hit.

"No kidding. I should've eaten less seafood," another guy cried out from farther away in his own personal agony.

And without missing a beat, my main man came howling out of the nuthouse to join the rest of us on our shitholes of shame.

Silence took over while the papaya seeds and senna tea combo moved mountains and monsters out of our butts. By the time the sun rose, we'd all found ourselves asleep, leaning against palm trees for relief. My fucking legs were sore, and I didn't have words to describe what my asshole was feeling like. I wasn't even sure if I had one anymore after shitting the entire night.

I looked up and slowly opened my eyes when I heard the sound of a soft bell and saw Gustoff standing there. I had no energy and no will to live at the moment, and Gustoff knew it.

"Congratulations on accomplishing *Apana Vayu*. This is one of the pranas in the body, of which there are five. The pranas are energies. *Apana Vayu* is situated in the rectum area and flows downwards. It is instrumental in discarding that which is unneeded. You must all feel a great accomplishment, knowing that your rectums have achieved a higher purpose in placing your bodies in a healthier state while expelling parasites and toxins that must be removed from our bodies."

"I'm proud I still have mine," Collin said the exact phrase I was thinking to myself.

"Very good. A positive phrase finally comes from the mouth of Dr.

Brooks," Gustoff said. "And yes, while all of you were beginning the first stage of your detoxification process, my staff and I researched your personal histories and the reasons you were recommended to our elite sexual intimacy program."

"Oh, God. I forgot we were here to revive the sexual intimacy in our marriages," I said with an exhausted laugh.

"Your orgasms will be much more intense now that the parasites have been flushed from your blessed rectums," Gustoff said, having a little too much fun insulting us when we were so vulnerable.

"I forgot that it's Christmas time. It's only three weeks away," another man said, bringing the holidays to my attention and how, instead of shopping or having holiday parties, I was hovering near a hole I had dug in the earth and filled with shit that dated back to my adolescent years. The man's response had nothing to do with what Gustoff was speaking about, but that's probably because he'd lost all sense of time and space after last night's harrowing ordeal.

"You will all feel one thousand percent motivated and thrilled to embrace the holiday season in any way you prefer," Gustoff added with a smile before ringing the bell again.

"What's the bell all about?" I questioned, still no energy to be combative.

"This is a Tibetan bell. It represents wisdom," he said, seeming much kinder now that I was thinking about it.

"That might be the wrong bell to be ringing on my account, Gus," Collin said, his voice weak and tired. "I think I expelled every ounce of wisdom with the *Apana Vayu* movements I was enduring last night," he said, prompting us to chuckle.

"Come," Gustoff said with a smile. "There are outdoor showers that flow naturally from our springs that will cleanse you all and prepare you for our yoga sessions today. The food that has been prepared will replenish your bodies from what was lost while flushing out the toxins."

"You know something?" Collin said, a man who'd practically begged to hold hands hours ago while the thunder rolling out of our asses slapped louder than any storm nature could drum up. "This might be good for us."

"You're dehydrated, lightheaded, and are *literally* no longer full of shit, so I'm guessing you really mean that?" I answered.

"I lost my will to fight, bro. I think I had an out-of-body experience last night," he said with a laugh while everyone fumbled to pull our tunics down and follow Rojak toward the showers.

"He got me a bit more interested after stating that this whole detox process will heighten the sexual experience. I'm going to need a payoff after that showdown last night," I said."Well, we have no idea what the next step will be, so let's not praise the detox gods yet."

"You think Ash and Laney had to go through this?" I asked, a bit concerned about my wife.

"Your wives are well looked after and taken care of, I assure you," the man leading us said. "Do not worry about them. Women are much stronger than men mentally. When you achieve ego death, you shall understand this."

"I'm not arguing with that truth," I answered. "I felt like I gave birth to a herd of buffalos, and I felt death coming for me last night. I've never imagined myself being stronger than my wife in such situations."

"Very good," the man smirked and smiled at me. "You may achieve ego death sooner than the rest."

"That's the hope," I said, proud of myself for scoring a point.

# CHAPTER 15

❄

Ash

After a rejuvenating spa day with a massage and cucumber water to help with hydration, I felt more relaxed and renewed than I'd felt in a long time. Granted, we could have done this at any luxury spa in Southern California, but to have the magnificent Indian Ocean to complement the scenery beyond our over-the-water villas? Well, nothing else could ever compare.

"Now, every holiday season, we cater to our lovely visitors and host a fun holiday boutique for you all to find and pull out that creativity that the stresses of your individual lives may have dampened. When you return to your rooms, you'll find the charm of our artificial trees, decorated with coastal ornaments and charm. You will also find paints and crafting materials to decorate ornaments from local shells and rocks there. Hopefully, you will use them to remind you of this special Christmas season you've chosen to spend with us on the island."

"Will our husbands be joining us for any of this?" a lady questioned with curiosity.

"Your husbands will be returning once they have gone through their rejuvenation process. After that, we hope they'll be reunited with their beautiful, relaxed wives and enjoy a few lovely nights with festive, renewed spirits," Hammond kindly stated. She raised her hands, guiding us to stand, "You are free to spend the rest of your days crafting or enjoying the healing salty air. All the food you need has already been delivered to your room. If you need anything more, you know how to reach us, and it will be delivered."

"This is heaven on Earth," Laney said, giggling and livelier than I'd seen her in months. "I bet the men regret bitching before they left now, too."

"True. They're probably ziplining and doing God knows what else in that forest they were brought to," I answered as Laney and I walked arm-in-arm to our neighboring villas. "So, what should we do?"

"I think we should go snorkeling again like yesterday, then lay out for a bit, and if you want, we can craft or whatever Hammond said." Laney chuckled, "I *know* you're dying to unleash your artistic side while we're here. I can't imagine a painter like you coming to a majestic place like this and being unable to unleash your talents."

"You know me well, don't you?" I laughed. "I love doing little crafts, too, especially with the kids." I took a deep breath and looked around at our surroundings, "It is weird though, isn't it?"

"What's weird?"

"Being in a tropical paradise when the Christmas season is starting? I love it, of course, but I'm afraid I won't be in the holiday spirit when we get home."

"I know what you mean," Laney answered. "And it does kind of suck that we came all the way out here to be at the *sex retreat* with the guys, and the first thing that happens when we get here is that they're taken away from us."

"Maybe they're going to learn some new fun tricks?" I teased.

"Dear God," Elena said. "What the hell do you think they're teaching them, and with what? Blow-up—"

I started laughing, prompting her to join in without saying anything more. "I don't think I want to know, and if the guys are dealing with blow-up anything, they're sure to be miserable on this trip. No, I think they're having a wonderful time hiking and doing guy stuff. If not, you know Jake and Collin. They would've already snuck back to us."

"That's true," Laney said.

WE WALKED into Laney's villa first, and I covered my mouth in shock.

"Oh, my gosh. Look at that gingerbread house," I said in disbelief. "It looks like a sandcastle version of the North Pole." I ran my fingers over the gumdrops and sugar-crusted roof, "This is incredible."

"Check out the tray of cookies," Laney said, walking over to the kitchen of her large suite. "Looks like we get to decorate them."

"Right here," I said, pulling a letter that looked written by Santa himself and reading it:

*In the art of island holiday cheer...*
*These are for you, Sweet Lady, while your man is not*
*near,*

*we invite you to decorate cookies of sweet delight,*
*for when your man returns,*
*he will have worked up a robust appetite...*

"Ooh," Laney hung onto the word sassily. "I'm pretty damn sure the appetite these guys will have worked up will have them craving more than cute, iced Christmas cookies."

"This is all very adorable, you know?" I said. "It's quite charming and very tropical North Pole-ish. Don't you think?"

"I do, and look at that Christmas tree," Laney said, chuckling and pointing across the dining area toward the living room.

The fireplace was lit, and the mantle above it was adorned with palm fronds and ferns to replicate the pine garland we were accustomed to. Soft white lights twinkled throughout the display that framed the healthy amber flames of the fire below.

As we walked toward the fireplace, a skinny artificial pine tree was decorated with ornaments made from seashells painted in Christmas colors. It was magical and encouraged me to feel more festive than before.

"It looks like the tree has a theme," Laney said. "Look, there's painted ornaments with horses and doctors. I'm guessing that's to represent our professions. And Collin loves sweets, so that must be why everything has this sugar-coated glitter on it."

"Hmm," I said, studying her room and taking it all in. "It is very *gingerbread sweets* in here. I wonder what mine and Jake's room is?"

"Let's go see," Laney said with the excitement of a child on Christmas morning. "What's Jake's favorite thing?"

"Jake loves everything," I answered. "What I'm curious about is how these people know Collin has a weakness for sweets?"

"Maybe the guys filled out a questionnaire when booking this sex retreat?"

I chuckled. "Look at us. We're on a sex retreat in *your* gingerbread

Christmas-themed room," I mused, knowing that our beloved CEOs had a lot to do with this. They kept me and Laney in a great mood while they pranked the hell out of Jake and Collin.

I just had to hope they didn't go too far over the top with whatever they'd planned for Collin and Jake.

"Oh, this is adorable," Laney said, walking into my villa. "It's a surf shop gingerbread house complete with a taco truck. Look at this," she said, pointing at the truck with a laugh. "They're gingerbread iced wheels."

"This is too funny," I said. "What about the tree?"

We walked into the living area, which was a replica of Collin and Laney's room, and looked at our tree. It was glittering and festive with painted tacos, surfboards, chips and guacamole, and jalapeño ornaments.

"I didn't realize Jake loved tacos and surfing so much," Laney said with a laugh.

"To be fair, he *is* obsessed with street tacos," I laughed. "It's so cute. Let's go back to your place and do ornaments there, and we'll ice cookies here tomorrow. What do you think?"

"I think this is the coolest thing ever. I didn't expect it, so I appreciate it that much more."

"Me, too. Who knows, maybe we'll be tasked to make homemade gifts for everyone later this week?"

Laney and I both fell into the sweet charm of enjoying the holiday season, even if we were in paradise and staying in a hut over the ocean water. Being inside the villas made us feel the holiday cheer. I missed Jake, but I also loved this. Doing handmade projects and making souvenirs to remember this darling holiday getaway was the icing on the cake for me. It was unexpected and appreciated. Isn't that what the holidays are all about, appreciating the unexpected and being delighted to gift simple treasures to your loved ones?

Well, that's what we were tasked to do: create tiny treasures for our husbands that would always remind them of what this intimacy retreat was all about—finding that spark again and the youthful glow we all had when we were first married.

# CHAPTER 16

❄

Jake

After gagging down fresh herbs, a tea that I still couldn't pin down the flavor on, and some watered-down, milky grass, I was shocked to feel a bit energetic again after last night's parade in the banana tree forest.

Thank God that nightmare was over, although I wasn't thrilled that it meant I was headed into the next phase of whatever-the-fuck this whole ordeal was.

"Feel your inner strength fighting its way to the surface, moving past the restrictions of this life and the troubles we face in it. Draw in the fabric of your essence and the raw power that propels you to…"

"Do you think this is going to help us like the breakfast we ate this morning that saved our lives after shitting all night?" Collin whispered to me as Gustoff spoke in some weird hypnotic voice in this group meditation we were forced into.

"I have no fucking idea. I just know that we better act like our egos died within four days from now, or we will be doing this for two weeks."

"I mean, I could try to get into this shit, but I can't focus with the way this man is talking. He's practically singing to us."

"I can't focus because my balls are resting on the dirt," I answered truthfully.

"Dr. Brooks and Dr. Mitchell," Gustoff called out, busting us like high school teens disrespecting the teacher during a lecture.

"Sir," I said in the most respectful voice I could muster.

I was a forty-year-old heart surgeon who could save this man without needing his gratitude or even a *thank you*. I needed nothing more than to see that he survived and lived another day to be with his family again. Yet, here I was, being treated like some sixteen-year-old piece of shit who'd been smoking weed in the parking lot before school.

"My name is Gustoff. I expect to be called that," he said in a resounding voice. "I do not appreciate the condescending names of a world that chooses to put people on pedestals, reducing them to mere titles in a farcical hierarchy," he said, making an example of me for referring to him in a manner I had been raised to use as a symbol of reverence.

"My bad," I said, holding back my annoyance at being used as the *bad student* example. "I just thought it was more respectful—"

"You *thought*, Dr. Mitchell," he answered, "and that was your first mistake. Thinking has led you down the wrong path, keeping your ego alive and your renewal unable to occur in the meditation that all of us, except you and Dr. Brooks, have chosen to take seriously."

"I'm taking this seriously, or I wouldn't be here with my balls and my wife's favorite physical treasure floundering on the dirt," I said.

No one laughed except Collin. I smirked over at him, thanking him with a smile for being on my team.

"Forgive me if this insults you, but when your wife filled out her questionnaire and was asked about the favorite attributes of her husband, your penis was never mentioned," he said, almost too happy in response.

"Well, my wife wouldn't say that to strangers. I'm sure she said it was my eyes or something cute," I countered.

"No, your eyes were never mentioned. It is strange that she wouldn't say that since she is a deeply spiritual woman who knows that eyes are windows to the soul."

I glared at the man, and I wished I could kill *his* ego instead of him harassing mine until it croaked. Fuck. If this was ego death, I didn't want this shit. More and more, I was willing to take Collin up on escaping this freakshow, going to rescue our wives from the hell they were most likely enduring, and getting off this fucking nightmare island.

"As I stare into your eyes from this distance," Gustoff continued, "I feel a darkness there that must be brought forth."

"The only darkness is me being highly irritated that my two-week Christmas break is being spent here with you, shitting in a hole in the forest, and the worst part is that I don't even have my beautiful wife in my arms."

"Good response, man," Collin said, knowing I was about to take more shit from this guy. The humor and drama from my interaction were more entertaining than the meditations we'd interrupted, so Collin was all about this happening at my expense.

"Thanks," I thanked him anyway because, facing facts, I needed the positive reinforcement.

"No problem," he winked at me.

"It is easy to see there are still toxins that were not depleted from your energy field during your *Apana Vayu* sessions," Gustoff said, nodding toward an assistant, giving him the go-ahead to dose me up on papaya and senna again.

Fuck that shit.

I stood. "Listen," I held my hands up in peace toward the man I'd internally declared an enemy, "I am in no way, shape, or form holding onto darkness like you believe you've seen in my eyes." I glanced around the room to the men who sat in subjugation because they didn't want to end up shitting in holes all night again. Most people used their damn brains and went along with stupid shit like this, but I didn't. I'd had about enough of Gus and the friendly meditation prison I was in. "And for the record, my wife *loves* my penis, so there's that, too."

"Jesus Christ, Jake," Collin feigned horror and shock. "Take it down a notch."

I eyed my best friend with annoyance, "Really, Collin? You're buying into all this?"

"If it saves my ass, and I mean literally, then yes." He whispered before he looked at Gustoff, and the meditation police who stood on stage with him, and pointed at me, "This guy is like a brother to me, but I don't agree with anything he's saying *at all*."

"Betraying a brother?" Gustoff said, seeing straight through Collin's bullshit.

"No," Collin said.

"Bullshit," I answered. "You're kissing ass to save your own because you know they're getting ready to hand me mine."

"Please rise and join your friend, Dr. Brooks," Gus said, making me borderline terrified about what would happen next.

"I'm good," Collin said. "In fact, I'm like you. I don't need the titles and whatnot like you were saying earlier. I would rather you keep me on your level and refer to me by my first name. Call me Collin. My patients and staff at the hospital refer to me as a doctor, as if I am above them, but there is no need for you to do so. We are all on the same level out here in this astounding yoga and meditation clinic."

"It's an intimacy retreat, Collin," Gustoff corrected my kiss-ass best friend, and I couldn't help but laugh at Collin's sleazy treachery, selling me out so that he didn't have to shit in a hole again. "And being a doctor is a noteworthy profession. Have you saved lives in your work?"

"I have, sir—I mean Gus. I mean Gustoff," he said, pulling himself together.

"This is a wonderful service to mankind and humanity; would you say so?"

"Absolutely," Collin answered, probably believing that Gus wasn't about to nail him in some unexpected way.

I didn't jump to his defense, even though I knew this was headed for disaster; his Judas act had earned him whatever was to come.

"Then why would you not seek acknowledgment for this? Why would you dare make so little of something so remarkable?"

"Well, I think it's because my ego has died," Collin said, giving his lying ass away.

"Your ego has died?" Gustoff said.

"Yeah. It happened last night while contemplating death during the *Apana Vayu* I experienced. And because of that, I seek no recognition or status in this world," he drew his hands out as if he were in some meditative class and waved them from hip to hip like he was creating a rainbow, "I am merely an average person like everyone amongst me."

"An average person, you say?"

"Yes," Collin answered.

"So, if you see yourself as an average person who has saved lives, do you consider those lives average as well?"

"Huh?" Collin answered.

"It is a simple question for an average mind like the one you claim to have, Collin," Gustoff said.

"Well, their lives weren't average. They were important, and those people mean something more to those who know and love them."

"But you insult them all by telling me they trusted an average man like yourself to save their lives," Gustoff said.

"No. Wait, what?"

"You just referred to yourself as an average person. Did you not?"

"Yeah, but that's not what I meant. I didn't mean to insult my patients or their families by saying they were average for choosing me as their doctor."

"That's exactly what you just declared," Gus answered.

"Quit while you're ahead, guy," I advised Collin.

"Well, I see them as the bright lights," Collin kept trying to dig himself out of this hole. "They did their research on me as their physician and trusted me to be their servant in saving their lives."

"You feel you were their servant. That is a blessed way to think for a seasoned doctor," Gus said.

Collin sighed in relief. "Thank you, and it's truly how I feel," he said, looking at every man who was staring at these two clowns.

"Do you charge money for your services, or should I say *servitude?*"

"Well, of course. Everyone knows you've got to pay the doctor, and the doctor has to eat."

"This is where your ego has deceived you, and your arrogance shines brightly tonight," Gus smiled. "You speak lies to get through this program. That's not at all uncommon," Gus glanced around the room. "Most men who are disconnected from their true sense of self lie and deceive and play games." He looked at me, "They are quick to anger and slow to forgiveness. Dr. Mitchell and Collin have shown us a valuable lesson, one we must always be mindful of."

"And that is?" Collin said, his mood now matching mine.

"Deceiving the ones trying to help soothe you and your spirit is merely deceiving yourselves. You hurt only yourself by lying through your teeth to progress through this program."

"That's the thing. I love my wife and my kids," I said honestly. "This trip was supposed to be a fun retreat. I thought we'd be firing up the sex life on all cylinders, but here I am instead in some weird-ass situation, feeling like a child who is getting busted for talking in class. I swear, I didn't sign up for this shit."

"No, you didn't. Your wives signed you up," Gustoff looked at Collin and me. "I knew you two would be the most difficult among us because the other men signed up for this themselves."

"So, my wife knew I would be going through this?" I answered, a bit disturbed that Ash would go so hardcore on my ass.

Shit, remind me never to miss John's band recital again.

"They knew you would all be reunited with more intense love and passion," Gustoff said. "Before we go further in our outdoor therapy, which will be braiding palms, I want to acknowledge that I am quite impressed with Dr. Mitchell and Collin today. Collin has shown me motivation, whether based on deceit or not, and Dr. Mitchell has shown me that he is progressing toward ego death by relating himself to his youthful inner child." He clapped his hands, "Good work today to the both of you."

I looked at Collin as if he'd grown two heads and then back to Gus as if he'd grown three. This was only day one of this circus, and I already wasn't sure what kind of man I'd return to Ash as. I was exhausted, hungry for a rare steak, and dying to be home. I would give just about anything to be at home and decorating for Christmas with Ash. Hell, I'd even put on a goddamn apron and bake fucking Christmas cookies. All the things I usually took for granted sounded like paradise right now.

My mind went to Ash, wondering if she was enjoying herself. She loved the holiday season, Bing Crosby playing in the background while she and the kids baked cookies and fudge and decorated the tree. Half the time, I referred to her as Mrs. Claus because she went all-out for the holidays, starting the day after Thanksgiving. Now, we were separated on this remote island, and it didn't feel like the holidays. To make matters worse, she couldn't decorate anything or bake cookies with the kids because we were here killing our egos.

I had to make this up to her. She was probably coming off the back of shitting in the sand all night while eating grass and participating in things that pulled her farther away from the festive brightness of the holiday season.

Instead of feeling sorry for myself, I became concerned about ruining the holidays for Ash by coming here and greedily thinking I'd be screwing my wife for two weeks straight to bring some fiery passion back to our lives. All she would've wanted was just to have me present while decorating the family Christmas tree, but instead, we were here. I had no idea how miserable my lady was on the other side of this island. Maybe tonight, if we didn't drink the shitting poison, Collin and I could escape and get back to the ladies. I'd book our flights home, and we'd be there in time to decorate and enjoy our children and families.

Because at this rate, with Collin selling out and not getting my back to save his own, he and I would wind up mortal enemies by the end of everything. Somehow, I felt responsible for saving Christmas… and I would.

# CHAPTER 17

❄

Ash

We were officially on day four of this relaxing and rejuvenating retreat, and I was ready for the men to return. I was fully refreshed and couldn't wait to show Jake and Collin the adorable ornaments Laney and I crafted yesterday after a relaxing two-hour massage, facials, manicures, and pedicures. This place was paradise for an exhausted mom like me; however, I missed my husband, and the buzz was that they may return tonight or tomorrow.

"Are we going for morning yoga?" Laney asked after we finished eating another delicious breakfast that this place spoiled us with.

"Why don't we skip yoga and meditation classes and finish the ornaments? Then, we can take the kayaks out after that. What do you think?"

Laney nudged me in my side, "You, skip meditation?"

I smirked. "You all give me a hard time about being into all this stuff, but I'm not rigid about it. I just like to keep myself grounded and centered when I'm stressed, which happens to be often when I'm home," I laughed. "Being here seems like a meditation on its own, you know?"

"I get that," Laney said. "I have to say I like meditating now that I've gotten the hang of quieting my mind."

"It's easy to do it at a place like this," I said, glancing at the light aquamarine water.

"It is," Laney answered as we walked along the wooden dock-like walkway that led to the entryways of our over-the-water villas.

"So, what should we do?" I asked when we got to the front of Laney's place.

"Let's finish the last of the ornaments we were making for the kids. After that, I'd love to get into my bikini and kayak," she said while I followed her inside.

"This place is so cute, but I'm going to get cheesy for a second and say I wish the guys were here to enjoy it with us," I said, sitting at the table where our ornaments and paints sat out from the previous day.

Laney sat across from me. "I know. I feel bad saying this," she cringed, "but I'm getting kind of bored. I'm ready for Collin and Jake to get back."

"Who knows whether they will come back today," I answered, dipping my paintbrush in the cobalt blue color and sliding it gently down the side of the starfish I was painting. "From how we're getting pampered over here, I'm confident the guys are being spoiled rotten on their side of the island with ziplines and who knows what else."

A knock at the door startled us both. I immediately wondered if the men were finally back, and I felt a jolt of excitement course through me at the thought.

"Avery? Nat?" I heard Laney say with her usual giggle of excitement.

I bolted up from the table and rushed to the door to see my best friend and Nat hugging Laney as they entered the villa.

"Ash, darling," Nat pulled off her oversized, gold-rimmed Versace sunglasses, and her blue eyes dazzled with her usual daring expression. "You look radiant!" she said, pulling me in for a hug before I could say anything.

"Babe?" Avery offered an adorable smile, piercing clear-blue eyes beaming beneath her black fringe bangs. "You look fully refreshed. We'll have to inform the Hawk brothers that their pitch to Jim and Spence was a brilliant idea."

"What do you mean?" Laney asked as I finished embracing Avery and stepped back in confusion.

"Yes, well," Nat said, eyeing the villa, "I suppose the whole *Christmas-themed* version of this could've been taken down a notch." She smiled at Laney and me, who stared at the women with confused expressions. "You know, *usually* when couples do meditation retreats —or sexual retreats, as was my recommendation—the husbands typically stay with their wives. Kind of difficult to have sex when one partner is gone."

"What the hell is going on here?" I asked before Laney could.

"Don't hate us for this," Avery said, "but we didn't want to tell you two what the guys were planning to get Jake and Collin back for the last nutty prank they pulled because if you two knew?"

"We needed you gals to have complete deniability," Nat said nonchalantly.

"What have you done?" Laney questioned nervously.

"I know it might feel sinful around the holidays," Nat started, "but it was to last no more than four days, and while this silly little prank went on, you two were both to experience what Titus and his brothers pitched to Jim and Spencer after they invested in this *Hawk Enterprises* resort."

"Can you stop speaking in riddles and tell us exactly what you planned," I answered. "Did Jim and the others ruin Christmas for Collin and Jake by sending them to what they believed was a sexual retreat?"

"Well, if Jack was convincing enough, then no," Avery said.

"Who is Jack?" Laney asked.

"Oh, that's right. You probably know him as Gustoff, but his real name is Jack," Avery continued. "If he's been convincing enough, Jake and Collin will likely be returned to you both as two of the most spiritual beings on the planet," she chuckled.

"I can see the looks on both your faces, and I know you're upset you weren't made aware of this," Nat went on. "That is why the next part of this Christmas vacation we're all joining you on will be replete with holiday cheer, Santa, his elves, and Jakey popping the cork and serving us all champagne in his adorable monkey suit. This was just a fun little gag for those two. So, let us fill you in," Nat said.

"Unless you both want to stay in the dark in case Collin and Jake think you're in on it too?" Avery said.

"Too late for that," I said. "Besides, they've only been gone for four days. Sure, they came here for sex, but I don't think they'd be *that* pissed for having to leave us for a few days."

"Let's just say Jake and Collin are experiencing a completely different version of this amazing vacation than you two," Nat said, pulling a laptop out of her bag and opening it. "Come here."

"Now, don't lose your shit when you see this," Avery said to us. "You'll notice that this is all being recorded live, and you may recall Jake and Collin doing something similar to Jim, Alex, and Spence?"

"Oh, yeah. When they did that survivor prank on them and stole all their camping gear while they were sleeping in the tents?" I questioned. "They recorded the entire thing, and they left the men with only the one set of clothes they had—"

"Sweats and long johns," Nat interrupted me with a laugh. "They hung cameras throughout that campground to make them truly believe they were lost in the wilderness with *nothing* but the clothes on their backs."

"That was a good one," I said, remembering Jake showing us the documentary at Jim's birthday party and how Jim was hilariously trying to rub sticks together to light a fire. "They did good, give them credit," I teased.

"They did *so* well that those men have been plotting revenge ever since. Now," she pointed at the laptop, "this is a live view of why we were questioning whether you two wanted to be aware of things."

I walked over to the table, and for any other group of friends, this might be unforgivable, but not for us. The men in our friend group were like toddlers when it came to shit like this. I could see now why

Laney and I were being pampered beyond any woman's dream. They wanted to keep us busy. I was almost afraid to see what these men were putting Collin and Jake through, all while watching their reactions in real-time.

"Now," Nat said, her nude polished acrylic pointing at a group of shirtless men sitting around some carved pole, legs crossed and palms facing up. "Everyone here, from the meditation instructors to the men in the audience, are all a hired group of actors," she said, smirking back at me. "Although a trained spiritualist was consulted for various things, including herbal teas and the food they ate, so they knew what they were doing," she chuckled.

"Oh...my God. What the hell did you guys do?" Laney said as we both looked closer. Everyone was wearing bright yellow loincloths, and Jake and Collin appeared to be in their own personal meditational zone within this bullshit scripted play.

"I can't believe Jim hired actors," I said.

"I know. You could've done this even better than them," Avery playfully nudged me, "but those two goofballs would've never taken it seriously."

My eyes widened as I watched the camera zoom in on Collin and Jake humming loudly, and I shook my head. "I want to laugh, but this is horrible," I said.

"This is Jake, Jim, Collin, Alex, and Spencer," Nat said with her eyes rolling, "and Collin and Jake had to know this would eventually come full circle and bite them in the ass."

"Wait. Shh," I said when the instructor—or should I say *paid actor*—started to talk.

*"Very well done. Now, as we center and ground ourselves to manifest our desires, I want you to call out to your inner boy, and ask for what you truly need, not want," the man said.*

"That's Jack playing Gustoff, a character designed to become Jake and Collin's nemesis," Avery said. "He's been orchestrating everything from the beginning."

"There's going to be fireworks when they learn Jim and the guys did this," Laney said truthfully.

"Totally," I covered my mouth, trying not to smile when I watched all the men stand up and do the yoga *tree pose*. "Okay, fill us in on everything from the second this was planned, put into place, and we got thrown into the action. And God help us all if the second part of this vacation isn't—"

"You girls better just be ready for some wild and rehabilitated spiritual men to rejoin you," Nat said with a chuckle, "because you're about to get two of the horniest and happiest assholes on the planet." She laughed at her joke while I stood in disbelief that Jim, Alex, and Spence had *actually* gotten those two tricksters back.

Nobody got one over Jake and Collin, but from the looks on Jake and Collin's faces, they'd been beaten at their own game. If Jim and the guys were watching this live like we were, they had to be crying with laughter at how seriously Collin and Jake were taking their hired actors.

I truly hoped they had some form of backup plan for this *vacation* because Jake and Collin would not hesitate to retaliate, and this would end up being some Nightmare Before Christmas situation, which would probably last until next Christmas.

I wasn't sure what would result from this doctor versus CEO game, but I could see Jake's youthful and relaxed expression, and it made my heart swell with love. Even though he was being duped, he went along with it, and I knew in my heart it was because he was trying his hardest to get through whatever they were being forced into so he could get back to me.

# CHAPTER 18

✻

Jake

Day four of what I was now referring to as *Holiday Hell* was upon us, and Collin and I had made plans to bolt tonight. Sadly, this lovers' retreat, or whatever this hellhole was called, was more of a torture than a help in assisting me to find inner peace or whatever I was expected to be looking for.

That ego death thing? Yeah, Collin and I could safely say that our egos had crashed, burned, and been incinerated after two nights of shitting in the woods to clear toxins and parasites from our bodies.

This was a literal shit show and something only dumbasses who cheated on their wives should be subjected to in order to save their marriages—not the ones who came here to keep the fucking spark alive.

"With the energy you're feeling while you chant, move your thoughts in the direction of that which you should like to manifest," Gustoff resounded the weird fucking chant we'd been listening to for the last hour or so. "Feel your soul call to it. Feel the crisp air surrounding your nearly naked bodies." I reopened my eyes, glanced at Collin's aggravated expression, then looked up to see Gustoff bang the dong to round out the bullshit he was spouting off. "Feel the goodness of life moving toward you like a rushing wave, mightily and boldly claiming the sands of the shoreline and taking what it wants. Your manifestations want you. They need you. They thank you for all your hopes and desires of them."

"Yes," I heard a man cry. "Yes, I need and want you."

"Fucking hell," I whispered to Collin, who was doing a fine job of pretending he was into this as much as I was.

We started faking interest in this bullshit after two nights to prevent another evening of shitting our lives away in the forest. In fact, we had been faking it so well that Collin and I had become Gustoff's two favorite husbands at this retreat.

"Shh," Collin said, his tone reminding me that if I did anything to blow our cover, we wouldn't be able to sneak out of here tonight. "Focus."

"Dude is moaning and practically orgasming right now," I said, feeling disgusted by Harold getting off in this manifestation thing we were stuck doing for the entire day.

"I'm going to sound just like him when I see Laney tonight, too," Collin said in a hushed voice, smirking before his face fell serious again as if he were deep in manifestation mode.

"Let us stand," Gustoff said, and everyone rose as if we were in some weird cult. "Dr. Mitchell," he nodded toward me, "Collin," he said with the usual approving grin he'd been giving Collin and me since we became his favorite kiss-asses.

"Yes?" I said as respectfully as I could.

"How are your souls this fine morning? I see you are both ever-so-deeply into this manifestation, and I trust you are feeling close to the harmonic balance of Mother Earth?"

"The peace is coursing with the magnetic pull and energy of the earth," I bullshitted him in response. "Mother Earth is bountiful in peace and stillness, and I accept it."

"I am grounded as well," Collin said, eyeing me because I took it a bit too far.

"I see this in the youthful glow you two are radiating today. A transformation has taken place, and your manifest power is overwhelming."

"You can feel that?" I blurted out without thinking.

"I feel energy," Gustoff answered, eyeing me skeptically. "I feel yours and Collin's stronger today than I have since you arrived; however, your vibrations seem slightly off. What is this I am sensing?"

*Goddammit. The bastard must be catching on to us.*

"My vibrations are strongly connected to Mother Earth and the magnetic pull—"

"It's like a hunger is trying to come forth," Gustoff said, interrupting me, "an urgency?"

*The only thing I'm hungering for is my wife and a rare fucking steak*, I thought, trying to stay focused.

"I only hunger for more of the peace and solitude this island has given us already," I answered.

"And you, Collin?" Gustoff questioned.

"The hunger I feel is a strong desire to be closer to Mother Earth," he sang back.

"Beautiful," Gustoff responded. "Then we have selected both of you to lead our fire mantras and chants on the shore tonight while the moon is full. Tonight, we will make camp on the shoreline. We had planned to return you to your wives this evening, but upon further assessment, no one is as far along in their ego deaths as Collin and Jake. We are not all in one accord," Gustoff eyed everyone around us. "If Dr. Mitchell and Collin were able to achieve this much peace and ego death in such a short time, it shames my heart to know the rest of you haven't accomplished the same. We must all attend the fire class, and tomorrow, we shall reassess everyone. Hopefully, you will return to your wives after that."

Gustoff disappeared with his men, who waited on this outdoor wooden stage, and we knew the routine from here. Once Gustoff was done with his instruction, he abruptly vanished, and we returned to *base camp* for directions on where we'd go next. We'd successfully done this more than a dozen times, and every time we were instructed to do some weird bullshit like braid palms, stack rocks, and tie knots in ropes.

"What the *fuck* are we going to do now?" Collin asked, reading my mind.

"Endure this bullshit for another night?" I answered. "Why does this seem like a prison?"

"Because that's exactly what it is, and I can't fake this shit another night," Collin said.

"Me neither," I answered. "I'm already accidentally thinking like that weirdo."

"No shit. After I felt bad for pissing on a tree this morning, I knew this was starting to fuck with my mind," Collin said with a laugh.

"Well, Gustoff would tell you that the tree was helping you by absorbing the toxins from your urine and—"

"Listen to you," Collin said. "The fact that you know that—That *I* know that—is a fucking problem."

"All right. This is what we'll do," I said. "Tonight, after we howl at the moon or whatever the fuck Gustoff is going to make us do to help the other dumbasses, we'll wait until they all fall asleep and then sneak the fuck out of here."

"Actually," Collin smirked, "maybe it's a good thing he's making us go to the beach. We can find our way back to Ash and Laney much easier."

"True. In fact, this may be *part of the journey*," I mocked Gustoff's favorite phrase, "and going to the ocean symbolizes us returning to where the ladies are. He's just got to have one more night of fucking us over."

"Is this the type of thing Ash is into?" Collin asked.

"No, thankfully," I answered truthfully. "Although I thought the same thing when we first got here," I smiled, missing my beautiful wife so damn much. "Ash is *nothing* like this. She meditates, and *grounds herself*, but she's *nothing* like these people."

"Thank God," Collin said. "This is weirding me out. It's like a cult. I wouldn't want to have to rescue Ash from something like this and rewire her brain," he laughed.

"I heard *that*," I agreed. "No worries there, although I feel like rescuing her right about now. I fucking miss her."

"I feel that shit, son," Collin said. "Come on. Let's head back to camp, eat grass for lunch, and get ready to get back to them."

"I'm never coming to the Maldives again," I said. "This was a place I'd always wanted to visit, but now, *fuck* no. This is worse than being stranded on a desert island, knowing I would never be rescued."

"Would you come back if you knew you'd be staying in those villas where we *thought* we'd be staying?"

"I don't know, dude," I said, honestly. "This whole place is just a traumatic destination for me," I sighed. "I guess the hopeful part is that we haven't seen the ocean this whole time, so maybe there's a slim chance I wouldn't associate those bad-ass water huts with this fucking jungle prison."

"There's the Christmas spirit," Collin chuckled.

"Christmas spirit," I laughed in response. "How can you even think about the holidays right now?"

"Simple," Collin said. "I just keep singing Jingle Bells in my head to make it look like I'm meditating. If I don't, I'm going to have a hard time accepting that Christmas is right around the corner when we get home."

"This whole trip is ruining everything," I admitted. "It's hard enough to get into the Christmas Spirit during a normal holiday season, and this shit, which we're barely surviving, is making the holidays seem nonexistent."

"I'd give anything to see a goddamn mall Santa and a fake North Pole just to get some festiveness in our systems," Collin chuckled.

"No shit," I answered as we approached the tent that led to where they fed us grass for food. "We *have* to get the fuck out of here tonight. Then, after we get to the ladies, we get our asses to the airport. That's when I'll call Jim and tell that bastard to get us the fuck off this island. His stupid ass better have a fantastic explanation about this place. I swear, if he and the guys set this up, knowing what was in store for us?"

Collin smiled, "Oh, the payback we bestow on those miserable fuckers will be *far* worse than anything you and I have experienced."

"Let's just stay focused on one thing at a time. We'll question those bastards about this trip, which they were all a little *too excited* to send us on, after we get back home. For now, we plan to get back to Laney and Ash."

Gustoff and everyone could kiss our asses. Fire chants or no fire chants, tonight we were breaking out of this *Island Escape Room* and going home to our families. I learned enough in my short time away from Ash that all I wanted was her. I wanted to see her smile, to feel her wake up in my arms, and to hold her longer in bed because I knew if we got up, it would take all day to get her back in my arms again. The tiny things I'd taken for granted were things I'd give anything for now, and it took this ridiculous trip to prove it to me.

# CHAPTER 19

❄

Jake

Everyone sat in the sand around a small bonfire, watching as Gustoff sang and hopped around it in some bizarre version of a fire dance. I'd never actually seen anyone do a fire dance, but whatever I had imagined it would look like didn't come close to what I'd witnessed here tonight.

"Gentlemen! Gentlemen!" Gustoff said. I would bet my life the dude was stoned. "Bring your inner children forth and allow the boy in you to be set free," he sang.

"Dude's fucken drunk," Collin leaned over and told me. "We should slip out now. He'd probably never notice."

"I figured bro was wasted when he bent over and started singing with his ass cheeks like Ace Ventura," I chuckled at the recollection because, after all the shit we'd gone through with our *proper spiritual meditations*, Gus bending over and singing with his butt cheeks almost made the whole trip worth it.

"It's a bummer this had to happen tonight," Collin said, looking around at the rest of the husbands in the group who were still taking this seriously. "I think I'm starting to like the guy after this."

"Husbands and wives, wives and husbands," Gus said as if he were about to declare our freedom. "You've all joined the cause in furthering the betterment of your wives," his eyes widened as he looked directly at Collin and me, "for your *lives*," he said, belting out a laugh, "yet how can any of this be meaningful?"

"What the hell is he on, ayahuasca?" I said to Collin.

"Hell if I know. All I know is that I need some of that," Collin answered humorously.

"Collin!" he pointed to my best friend. "Stand, my good man. Stand and declare your love for Christmas!"

"What the fuck?" I said, laughing at this man's ridiculousness.

"Declare my love for my wife, you mean?" Collin answered. "Because trust me, my good, inebriated native, she is worth more than a holiday to me."

"Ah," Gus answered. "This is true!"

He giggled, and that's when Collin's mischievous grin appeared. For the first time since we'd been subjected to this torture, my partner-in-crime reemerged, and a sense of revitalization coursed through my veins. We could have a lot of fun with this guy since he was dumb enough to get fucked up.

"And how about you, Gus?" Collin said, all sense of faking it from the last three days vanishing into the salty air. "Are you married?"

"Married? Me?" Gus looked at me. "Dr. Mitchell, stand! Arise, good doctor!"

"Gus—"

"You joined us to bring back the love in your marriage. Is this true?"

"The love never left, my man," I smiled confidently, knowing that was true.

"Then why are you here?" Gus asked, his expression showing that he probably had forgotten what we were discussing.

"He came here to fuck his wife," Collin said, enjoying Gus being drunk too much. "In fact, that's why we're all here."

"You all came here to fuck my wife?" I teased Collin's unfortunate turn of phrase. "If I'd have known that—"

"What? No, stupid," Collin said, thrown off his game after he realized how his words came out. "I meant my wife. Not everyone— Goddammit, everyone came to fuck their own individual wives, okay?"

"I hope Ash will be able to contain her disappointment," I shrugged as Collin laughed. "Back to the point, Gustoff," I redirected my attention. "We didn't sign up for whatever the hell we've gone through the past few days."

"That's intriguing," Gustoff suddenly seemed to sober up. "It's intriguing that you've both proven that there has been no ego death between you."

"Are you fucking with me?" I nearly barked at the man's instant transformation.

"No," he answered. "That you both thought you could go unnoticed and toy with my program is beyond me. You will now be taken to another location to meditate amongst the forest and stars to beg forgiveness."

"I'm not fucking going anywhere, and I'm not begging for jackshit," I snapped. "You know what? I lied. I *am* going somewhere. I'm going back to my wife and getting out of this place."

"You cannot," Gus informed.

"Last I checked, we were the ones paying for this fucked-up retreat, and as paying customers, we're fucking done with this nightmare," Collin said.

"Gentlemen, stop them," Gus said with a roll of his eyes and a wave of his hand.

As if we were in some horror film, Collin and I were grabbed from behind and bags were pulled over our heads. Before I could react, my hands were tied behind my back with ropes, and I was being dragged somewhere.

The only thought running through my head was for Ash and Laney. The possibility that they were going through this, too, gripped my heart so tightly that I thought it would choke me. My heart was racing, adrenaline coursing through me as Collin and I were dragged and eventually planted onto some ice-cold chair.

"Take off their covers," I heard a voice say.

"Fuck you," I heard Collin snarl in return.

The next thing I knew, the cover was taken off my and Collin's heads, and a genuine fear that we had just been kidnapped for ransom shook me to my core. If they could do this to Collin and me, I couldn't think about what they'd do to Elena and Ash. My sweet wife had been through so much. This was all my fault.

"Where's the big guy?" a young man asked.

"The big guy?" I questioned.

"Yeah, the one who insisted we retrieve you so he could question you," the man answered.

"Listen, I have no idea what you guys want, but I'll pay you off before *the big guy* can get here."

"Sounds enticing, but Big J is paying us a lot more for your bounties than you could," he cackled like a proper scoundrel.

"Bounties?" I looked at Collin.

"Oh, I don't know. I'd pay a pretty price for your ass," Collin shrugged, unaffected by this scenario, which gave me a bit of relief. Maybe I'd overreacted?

I eased up immediately and smirked at him. "I'd give those assholes a hundred thousand for your cute ass," I teased.

"A hundred thousand? You were going to give a million for Sebastian's at that bachelor auction," Collin said. "I thought—no, I *know* I'm sexier than that son of a bitch."

"Well, what would you give these chumps for me?" I asked.

"Two hundred thousand, but that's *only* because you didn't come up with our escape plan earlier," he said.

"Me?" I answered. "I didn't see you coming up with any bright ideas while we were shitting our brains *again* the second night here."

"Oh, no. Did you guys drink the water?" a man asked curiously.

"No," I answered him.

"They drank the senna tea and ate the papaya as *Gustoff* suggested," I heard my brother's voice humorously say as he, Alex, and Spencer entered the small, enclosed area we were in. "Hey!" Jim said with a smile bigger than Santa's on Christmas Eve. "Merry Christmas, dipfuckers."

"What the fuck!" Collin and I said in unison.

"Payback is a bigger bitch than karma sometimes, eh?" Jim snickered.

I had no words. All Collin and I could do was silently stare at the men who'd been victims of so many of our ruthless pranks.

The day had finally come when they'd gotten us back.

Shit, I think I was prouder of my brother for being so creative than I was pissed off at him for having the nerve. Although being proud of him would fade quickly, and Collin and I would get our retaliation.

The most important thing I needed to know was how the hell they managed to pull this off on Collin and me, of all people.

# CHAPTER 20

❄

Ash

After Avery and Nat got Elena and me up to speed, I counted the minutes until I saw Jake again. While Laney and I had been pampered the past few days, our husbands had been masterfully pranked, but Avery and Nat assured us it would end with a delightful *Christmas surprise.*

After watching the *live feed* of the men enduring that bonfire meditation with the hired actor Jack, playing a guru named Gustoff, I had no idea what mood Jake would be in after he found out his brother had orchestrated the entire trip. It was difficult to believe anyone had gotten one over on Jake and Collin, let alone Jim. I guess it shows that after decades of Jake pranking his brother, Jim had enough and finally got his revenge.

Jake and Collin had just discovered that this was a joke at both of their expenses and while I wished I were a fly on the wall in that room right now, I was more concerned with putting on this skimpy *Mrs.*

*Claus* outfit and distracting my man from unleashing hell on his brother and friends.

"Angel?" I heard Jake say as I finished pulling on the short skirt and clasping it in the back. "Where the hell are you?"

His voice was filled with relief and humor as I entered the living room. I stopped, and my breath caught at how blue my husband's beautiful eyes were. The dark hair on his face from not shaving for four days was enough to make me swoon right then and there. Since I'd known the man, he hadn't gone more than a day without shaving. I'd never seen him like this before. He looked more masculine and robust than ever, and all I wanted was to feel his raw power inside of me.

"Hot damn, baby. You look amazing," I said, unable to contain myself as I rushed across the small space to be in his arms again.

"I probably smell like shit. I need to get cleaned up," he said while his lips moved from mine, and his tongue and mouth worked their way along my jaw and down the center of my chest. "Oh, God," he growled, his lips moving over my very pronounced cleavage, thanks to this bra, "I'm going to cum just tasting you."

"Jake," I panted, searching for oxygen and feeling more pleasure than I expected I would, knowing that we were about to have the most glorious sex we'd had in quite some time. "I'll get in with you," I breathlessly said, my hands running over the top of his head while his lips journeyed down the inside of my thigh.

"Glad you said it," he chuckled and scooped me up and into his arms, "because I'm not letting you go until we have made up for all this lost time."

I held onto Jake and giggled as he picked me up. I pointed toward the bathroom, and we wasted no time getting into the shower and escalating things. I returned Jake's powerful kiss, his tongue pressing hard and passionately against mine. Jake moaned as we slipped under the warm running shower, holding me in one arm and ensuring we didn't slip with the other.

I was so lost in my husband consuming my entire body that I

didn't even question how his clothes were already off, and mine were still on.

"Oh, shit," I snapped to reality, pulling my hungry lips away from Jake's. "This outfit," I chuckled.

Jake's passionate expression never changed, and I fell into a trance under his penetrating gaze as he ignored my worry about the velvet Mrs. Claus dress. He turned me around, pressing me against the wall as his hand went to the one place on my body that needed him the most.

The shower was drenching both of us as my head fell back against Jake's shoulder, and I pressed my ass against his hard dick. Thankfully, my mini skirt covered nearly nothing, and I had nothing on underneath, allowing easy access.

Jake stepped back. "I need to wash up, baby," he said. "I want to watch you get yourself off in this sexy little outfit."

I turned to face him, drinking in every part of my man's perfect body. The dark hair that covered his chest and the line of hair that led down to his large and perfect cock made me bite my bottom lip in hungry desperation for him to be inside of me.

I stood facing him while he smiled greedily at me as I turned this into a fun moment of stripping out of this soaking wet costume. I remained as seductive as I could, loving the moment we were having, while Jake began to wash up, and I started removing my top. Once my breasts were freed, my husband's eyes went to my hardened nipples.

"You're so beautiful, angel," Jake said, stepping toward me before his lips firmly captured mine. "I could take you right here and now, but I don't want the water to get cold," he chuckled, picking me up again. Then, in a rush of consuming kisses, we were once again lost in each other.

"I'm giving you your Christmas present early tonight," I said as I rolled Jake to his back and straddled him.

"Oh?" he said with a humored laugh. "What do you have planned, baby?"

Jake's head rested against the pillows as I pressed my hand against his chest, leaned forward, guided his cock to my entrance, and slid down the length of his shaft.

Jake's expression instantly changed with my unexpected response to his question, and he growled a moan that turned my ass on, making me want more. Feeling the intense satisfaction of Jake being inside of me forced me into a zone that wasn't where I usually played when it came to sex with this man. I became more dominant, loving that my body controlled him in a way that made me feel powerful.

His eyes became glossy as they locked onto mine, and his hands were limp around my waist as I moved up and down, his dick feeling the slickness and wetness of my pussy that had needed him for far too long.

"God, I love you," he whispered, in a trance almost as if he were high.

Jake's eyes rolled back as I steadied myself, clenching his hard dick with my pussy to keep his cock restricted with pleasure inside of me. Typically, Jake would be reaching my clit and helping to bring me pleasure, but this time, he had fully succumbed to the pleasure I was giving him. His soft whimpers, moans, and the gentle way he slid his tongue on his bottom lip, tilting his chin up with every move I made, were spurring me on and enticing me in ways I hadn't felt in far too long. I was about to come along with my husband, and I wasn't even touching myself.

I moved faster and faster as my impending orgasm built, and then I shifted myself so his dick hit my spot. Jake groaned in pleasure at the same time as I did when I moved his dick over the surface of my G-spot, and I couldn't stop now if I wanted to. A whole-body, internal shiver coursed through me, and my parched lips went straight to Jake's. His body and hands, which previously seemed numb to all these sensations, were strong and determined as we fell into this fervent rhythm.

We groaned through our powerful and desperate kiss, Jake sitting up while moving himself deeper into me. I dug my knees into the bed, feeling his cock burrow deep inside me, and we both cried out in an intense and mind-shattering orgasm.

I had no idea what my husband had gone through over the past four days, but starting our reunion like this, knowing there was more to come, proved that something was different.

And I liked it.

# CHAPTER 21

❄

Jake

After multiple profound rounds of unhinged sex with the beauty currently asleep in my arms, I was the happiest man on earth. Who knew it only took being held captive by that fucking actor, Jack, to achieve the feeling of what life would be like if I lost my lady and, of course, joined a cult.

Since opening the door to Ash's adorable little Christmas cottage, I hadn't thought about the bullshit my brother and our friends had cooked up for Collin and me to endure since we got here.

She moved in my arms, causing me to pull her in closer to my chest, wrapping myself tightly around her. That's when my fucking phone rang and wouldn't stop.

"For fuck's sake," I said, knowing if I didn't get the damn thing, Ash would wake up. "What?" I snapped when I saw it was Jim calling.

"Hey, the plane is taking off in two hours. You two had all night to reunite, and now—"

"Why are you calling to tell me this?" I said, pissed I had to slide out of bed and stand across the room butt naked, listening to my brother's smug voice.

"Because if I don't, your spiritual butt is going to be stuck here and taking a commercial flight," he said.

"That's fine by me. I'd prefer that and to spend the remaining—"

"You'd actually prefer commercial?"

"Yep."

"Look at you. Ego death suits you well, baby brother," he said, laughing at all the stupid shit he put me through.

"It's not ego death, asshole," I answered. "I fly commercial all the time, unlike your arrogant CEO ass."

"Well, that is true," he conceded. "Regardless, if you miss my jet leaving, you'll be on your way back to California for Christmas instead of where—"

"That's the thing with this amazing ego death trip I'm on now—"

"You say that as if you're on an acid trip," he interrupted.

"It feels like an acid trip, and if your crazy ass had gone through what I just experienced, you'd feel the same."

"Well, amazing or not, you'll not want to miss this flight because we have a genuine Christmas surprise for everyone to make up for the torture we put you and Collin through."

"Interesting. This happens to be the first year I prefer to spend it alone with Ash and *her family*, not my own. Have fun, and Merry fucking—"

"Well, you're going to be pretty bored after your long-ass flight home with Ash to find the two of you are spending it alone."

I closed my eyes and pinched the bridge of my nose, "How in the fuck did I manage to put myself at your mercy?"

"Relax, Jacob. You're officially safe," he said. "Now, Ash will not be leaving your side, and you'll be landing in Switzerland, where you'll be whisked away on a train that will take you to your kids and in-laws for—"

"Hold the fuck up," I said. "Let's skip over the fact that you sound like some fucking gameshow host, telling me what my grand prize is, and get to the part where you tell me how you're sending my kids and Ash's parents to Switzerland for Christmas. Are you joking?"

"Not joking," Jim said. "And most people would dream of spending the holidays there, fuck face. Jesus, I thought your anger issues were worked out in that meditation retreat, but maybe you need to go back?"

"I didn't realize I had anger issues until I spent two nights shitting in a hole that *I personally* dug for myself in the banana tree forest, then ate fucking grass and braided—"

I stopped when I heard Jim's explosive laughter and waited impatiently for him to catch his breath.

"Oh, fuck, man," he said. "I swear to Christ, I thought you and Collin would get out of there after the first night. I'm still shocked we got you guys all the way to the end," he laughed again, and I narrowed my eyes.

I was done being upset about this. My wife and I had seriously had the best sex of our marriage because of this whole thing, although I would never tell Jim that. Maybe detoxing years of shit in my guts made way for killer orgasms, and I wasn't mad about that anymore. However, Jim's smug laughter only urged me to think of how I would get him back. Collin and I hadn't had time to discuss our revenge, but it was sure to be epic after what we'd been through.

In the meantime, I figured it was prudent to keep quiet and pretend it was all water under the bridge; that way, payback wouldn't be expected. So, fine. Jim had some spectacular Christmas trip planned for all of us to spend together, and I know my brother when it came to things like this. He spared *no expense*. He would probably fly Santa himself in from the North Pole if it meant the kids would have an unforgettable Christmas. My brother had always been one happy little fucking elf during this holiday, and so I knew he went all out.

"Are you still there?" Jim questioned my silence.

"I am, and you know what? You're right. Collin and I had all that shit coming. We've done all of you dirtier than you did to us," I lied.

"That's what I hoped you'd conclude," Jim answered.

I rolled my eyes.

"I know, and I'm sure you also want me to admit that your stupid bullshit was worse than our pranks on you idiots?"

"Well, yes, but that is unnecessary," he said.

I glanced over to Ash, still sleeping soundly, her auburn curls neatly spread over my pillow where I was once lying fully relaxed in an after-sex, drunken stupor. We had to get our asses up and to Jim's jet if we wanted to see the kids, whom I missed terribly. Bullshitting with Jim and getting into these ridiculous pissing matches was doing us no favors in the time department.

"Listen, we'll tally the score later. I need to wake Ash. We'll meet you guys in the lobby of this place," I answered.

"All right. And, hey, the Hawk Brothers said that you and Ash are free to come again to visit their five-star retreat here anytime you wish," he said, taking another dig at me.

"I'll keep that in mind," I answered. "See you guys in about thirty minutes."

"Hey, Jake?" Jim said.

"Yeah?"

"Don't let Ash in on the whole trip just yet. This part is Avery's gift to everyone, and she wants the ladies to be surprised."

"How adorable," I mocked.

"It is, and when you see the train I rented and had decorated to look like the North Pole Express, you'll agree when I say it was worth every penny," he laughed.

"How much money did you pay to rent and decorate a fucking train?"

"Let's just say your brother isn't a successful businessman because I'm a fool," he answered, "because after we're done enjoying the damn thing, I convinced the company to give me a percentage of what they charge others to ride on it for the holidays."

"You went into the train rental business, eh?" I asked, confused.

"Don't work yourself up trying to figure it out," Jim laughed. "Just meet us in thirty minutes in the *welcome center*. That's what it's called, by the way. The welcome center, not the lobby."

"Thanks for correcting me on that," I said. "I wouldn't know. I haven't been here all week. I've been shitting in the woods."

That was enough of Jim for now. If we were all flying to Switzerland for the holidays, I would have enough time to talk with him on the way to our destination. I needed to wake my wife and get ready to enjoy her excitement, knowing that she was about to embark on a wonderful Christmas surprise that her best friend had planned.

# CHAPTER 22

❄

Jake

When we boarded the train that would bring us to our destination, I couldn't help but laugh at all the shit that had gone down up to this point. We'd officially gone from some whack-as-fuck meditation retreat planned by my brother and his buddies to riding on some remarkably decorated Santa Train and headed to St. Moritz in Switzerland.

This train was a sight to behold with all its elaborate Christmas décor. Red velvet seating was encased by ornately carved, rich mahogany wood with brushed gold accents in every nook, and freshly cut evergreens were fashioned into thick, fragrant garland. It felt like the train had ridden the rails straight out of the North Pole and brought its whimsical magic through Switzerland and the Swiss Alps. The ambiance was ideal, keeping everyone filled with holiday cheer and saving my brother's ass from my inevitable retaliation. He was lucky I was in such a festive mood.

I thought we'd be staying at one of the many luxury hotels where the rich and famous love to vacation when they're in this area, but my brother had other plans through all his *lovely* connections. As it turns out, the Aster family owned one of the first villas built in the upper St. Moritz area. From what Jim said about this historic chalet, it had ten bedrooms spread over five floors, and we were sure to find the best Christmas experience there.

"How much are the Asters charging us to enjoy their exclusive winter escape?" I questioned Jim as we sat in the lush velvet seating of the dining car on the Christmas train.

"Why would the Asters charge us to stay in their home?" Jim asked, sipping his heavily spiked eggnog.

I glanced around the ornately decorated train car where we sat, wishing Ash was enjoying it with me instead of napping in our plush train car, but after the night we'd had, my lady needed to catch up on her sleep.

"Well, Seb and John wouldn't, obviously, but their parents?" I said, sipping my eggnog from a silver mug. "I don't know. You businessmen tend to make money on everything you do." I reached for a lemon cake from the dessert platter in the middle of the table before us. "Like this train?"

"What about it?" Spencer chimed in with that damn smirk I'd seen him wear since convincing me to go on the *lovers' retreat.*

"Oh, please. Don't act like we were born yesterday," Collin said. "Jim didn't only do all of this shit for Avery, the kids, and the rest of the ladies." He arched his eyebrow at my brother. "You're probably only doing this because you're proposing some deal to the owners of this train to go into business and make a little side cash during the holidays."

"As they say, the wealthy stay wealthy because they don't blow their cash on bullshit," I said. "The Asters are not the type of family to do anything for people that doesn't benefit them in return."

Jim smiled at me in response to that, "So you're saying that Big Daddy and Margot Aster didn't do this out of the goodness of their hearts?"

"That's exactly what I'm saying," I answered him.

"Look at the mindfulness with which you come to these conclusions," Jim chuckled, the booze in his eggnog keeping him light and humorous. "You should go on those meditation retreats more often. It has expanded your conversations to more in-depth—"

"You start this vacation off by torturing us with a mindless *prank*, which you all," I eyed Jim, Alex, and Spencer all sitting around the dining car with smug grins on their faces, "should have been praying that Collin and I would forget about."

"Well, that's partly why you're on Santa's Express," Jim answered with a chuckle, eyeing his co-conspirators.

I couldn't wait until retaliation befell all three of these bastards just because of this ridiculous, *clique* vibe they were throwing out.

"And then you try to insult me by saying that Gustoff was paid to fuck with me and Collin—"

"Jack," Alex interrupted me with a chuckle.

"What?" I said, confused.

"The man that played the role of Gustoff is named Jack," he smiled arrogantly at me. "Jack Masterson. He's trying to get a big break in Hollywood and hoping *this* might be it."

"How the fuck is he supposed to get a big break in Hollywood when he's fucking around in the Maldives like some fake meditation guru to mess with Collin and me?"

Jim snickered, bringing me and Collin to stare at him with curiosity.

"Well, you should probably know that cameras documented everything you guys did and went through. We have all of it recorded." Jim flipped his phone, and my mouth dropped open when I saw the night vision cameras recording Collin and me out in the forest on the second night.

"You're not that fucking stupid," Collin said. "I swear to everything that makes Christmas *jolly and bright* that you will all pay dearly if you don't delete that off every single device."

"And *Jack Masterson* and I will have words if he thinks he's going to make it in Hollywood on our backs, being pranked by you three dickheads," I added.

"Here's the deal," Jim said, putting his phone down and offering us both that damn controlling CEO look. "All of this *insurance* goes away and gets deleted off of all devices once we're assured that you two won't retaliate."

I smirked at my brother. "Look at you three chicken shits." I eyed the smug executives. "Scared shitless about what Collin and I are going to do to get even."

"Of course," Spencer said casually. "It was a fun prank, nothing worse than what you two would do; however, you two don't like being fucked with the same way you fuck with everyone else."

"So, we knew that if we finally got your asses back for the bullshit you are relentlessly pulling on us, we'd have to do something drastic," Alex added, almost as if they'd all rehearsed this *mafia-style* conversation before putting their plans in motion.

"We knew we had to have insurance so you wouldn't retaliate. Thus, the recordings," Jim finished.

"I don't know about you," Collin said to me, "but I couldn't give a fuck what anyone thinks about us shitting our brains out in the woods."

I smiled at my best friend. "I agree. Actually, I think it's a fantastic way of reminding the world that everyone should do an annual colon cleanse. It's a healthy way for two surgeons to show the world that if we can do it, anyone can do it, and colon health is extremely important." I brought my cocky smile back to the three men trying to blackmail us.

"Where did you get the idea to blackmail us anyway?" Collin laughed with carefree ease.

"You two shitting in the woods isn't all we have recorded," Jim said, strangely still smiling. "Cameras were everywhere, even when your cute little faces were sound asleep and *talking* in your sleep."

"Who cares about talking in our sleep," I challenged. "Everybody does that. It's perfectly normal."

"You're right about that much," Spencer said. "However, *what* you two were cry-babying about while you slept makes the recorded material worth it in the end."

"I'm not taking that bait," Collin said. "You three are fucked. You're scared and have no idea when or where my boy and I will get you back."

I leaned back in the comfortable train chair, smiled, and crossed my arms, "Show the fucking videos to the world. Hell, Jack Masterson will be grateful to Collin and me for making him famous, but you three are fucked, and you know it."

"You're willing to let down the women and all the kids at Christmas just to get us back?" Alex questioned.

Collin grinned and leaned forward. "The only ones being let down will be you three. It was a dumb idea to prank us right before the holidays," Collin said, smiling back at me.

"It was even more foolish to attempt to blackmail us with your cheesy-ass videos," I added and then stood when Collin did.

We eyed the men cockily before leaving the three executives to ponder what Collin and I would do now.

"Insurance, my ass," Collin said as we left the dining car and walked into the lounge car filled with sofas, an adorable fireplace, and three Christmas trees to keep the festive appearance of Jim's North Pole Express flowing flawlessly throughout the train.

"Well, they are fucking scared. I mean, it's the first proper prank they were bold enough to play on us," I answered, walking over to the sofa and sitting down.

Collin sat in the deep red velvet chair to my left, facing the ornately carved wooden fireplace. "What should we do?" he questioned with excitement.

"This one is a hard one because it's the holidays, *and* if we get their smug asses back, it has to be impactful."

"Something that will teach them not to fuck with us, of course," Collin added, as deeply in thought as I was.

"Jim's right. We can't fuck up Christmas for the women and the kids," I said. "We have to play by the rules."

"Of course," Collin answered, "but let's think about it. We never fuck up things when we pull off our silly pranks on those assholes. In fact, the women enjoy it."

"We are a great time when it comes to shit like this," I said with a smile. "We can pull this off easily, and it will make for a fantastic Christmas that no one shall ever forget."

"But what are we going to do?" Collin said. "I mean, we're in Christmas Country. I don't know shit about anything in Switzerland."

"We'll do the only thing we can do," I narrowed my eyes at him. "We go balls deep with all this Christmas shit. One thousand percent Christmas spirit."

The lights went on in Collin's eyes, "Nothing like this Christmas train to inspire us to go all-out, obsessively covering every Christmas tradition known to man?"

"We can kick it all off by singing everyone's favorite Christmas tune by the Queen of Christmas herself?" I arched an eyebrow with a smile.

Collin raised his mug of eggnog toward me, "All I want for Christmas is *you*, baby!"

I tipped my mug to salute my best friend, knowing *exactly* what we were about to do. We were going to make these businessmen do every fucking Christmas thing that we could think of, forcing them not to open a laptop or check business numbers and holdings on their phones until we were done with them. Isn't that what all our lovely wives and children wanted from us lately anyway, to disconnect from everything keeping us from them? Well, this would be the Christmas miracle they've been dreaming about.

It was time these smug CEOs found their own form of ego death this Christmas, and Collin and I would happily and festively give it to them.

# CHAPTER 23

❆

Ash

Contrary to how my husband and Collin felt, spending the first part of this vacation in the Maldives was a perfect way to kick off the holidays. Even though we'd been in an island paradise, it was lovely to be pampered in a stress-free environment while making adorable Christmas ornaments that I couldn't wait to show the kids.

I initially worried that being on the island would take away from my holiday spirits, and even if that were a little bit true, the train we were riding had surpassed all my expectations when it came to immersing myself in the holidays.

I'd decided to take a quick nap, but I'd fallen into a deep sleep and woke up having no idea how long I'd been out. I was bummed, thinking I'd missed the whole train ride and all the gorgeous scenery that came along with it, but when I looked out the massive window to my left, I saw the majestic beauty of the snowy Swiss Alps and was overcome with serenity.

This train car was something else. It was like a suite on rails, decorated like a small, luxury apartment with a queen-sized bed, fireplace, and a beautifully decorated Christmas tree in the corner.

I sat up and moved to the chair by the fireplace, allowing my sleepy brain to wake up some more before I fixed my hair, changed clothes, and rejoined everyone in the other train cars.

I sat in the red velvet chair next to a small table with cakes and tea, situated by the window that framed the glistening, snowy white mountains and hillside we were traveling through.

"Gosh," I said to myself, taking the teapot and pouring myself a cup, "this is the most beautiful place I've ever seen." I smiled, choosing the peppermint tea bag to accompany the Swiss chocolates arranged on a tiny silver platter.

"It's gorgeous, isn't it?" Jake said, entering the room as I began talking to myself. "But you should know," he crossed the room and bent to kiss me, "none of this beauty compares to yours, angel." He sat in the chair on the other side of the small table filled with Christmas goodies.

I grinned at my husband's lively and excited expression, "It seems you're in much better spirits?"

He took a decorated Christmas cookie and bit into it with a flirty grin. "I've been in a much better mood since being reunited with my wife, especially after you and I went all night to make up for lost time in the Maldives," he said.

After all the years I'd known my husband, I prided myself on knowing all his looks. I knew the excited look he got on his face after great, satiating sex. I also knew the look he wore when he was thrilled to get away from work and take a vacation. And then there was *this* particular look. It was like a combination of excitement from having fulfilling sex, going on vacation, and, I don't know, getting a new sports car. It was the look of knowing he was about to exact perfect revenge on someone for trying to beat him at his own game. And I knew this look very well because he and his best friend were notorious for *getting each other back* at any cost.

"I see you've come up with a brilliant way to get Jim back," I said, not needing to question the sparkle of mischievousness in his vibrant blue eyes.

I sipped my delicious tea and smiled at him as he tried to cover up his expression, which was a dead giveaway.

"No," he brought a piece of dark chocolate to my lips, "I'm just happy."

I rolled my eyes that this man thought I would believe a lie from him after all these years of marriage.

I leaned back in my comfy oversized chair and glanced out the window again, taking in all the beautiful scenery. "You're just *happy?*" I asked, looking back at his calculating expression. I could only imagine what was going through his head.

"Absolutely, baby." He snapped out of his thoughts *of revenge* and smiled at me, "In fact, if you weren't just waking up, I'd prove that happiness to you on that Christmas-themed train bed."

"Jacob Mitchell," I said. "We've been married forever and a day. Do you think I'm going to buy into the fiction that you're *waiting for me to wake up* to have sex? No, my darling." I smiled at him. "The *only* thing that stops *you* from having sex with me is *knowing* you have a retaliation plan to enact on some poor soul for pulling a silly prank."

He eyed me skeptically. "That's not true at all," he lied straight to my face.

I sighed. "Listen, I have no idea what you and Collin have planned, but I've been in here sleeping *uninterrupted* for at least three hours, which has given you two more than enough time to mastermind something. So, here are the rules I am enforcing *if* you and Collin are up to no good with your revenge plans."

"Rules?" Jake chuckled. "Baby, I always follow the rules, unlike my brother, who went completely outside of them by ruining our vacation."

"Jim didn't break any rules," I laughed. "Why else do you think Elena and I were so relaxed and well taken care of while they got you two goofballs back for all the shit you've done to them?"

"So, you're saying that you were perfectly fine not seeing me for four days when you expected that to be a *sexual* retreat?"

"I'm saying that you and Collin were beaten at your own game, and I know that will never sit well with you. I also know the look of the devil in your eyes right now. I know you and Collin will not stop until all the men who had any part in getting you back are paid in full for even *considering* pulling one over on you two," I eyed him, feeling like all I was doing was encouraging him more.

I couldn't help but laugh at this man I was so deeply in love with. He was so serious, brilliant, and commanding in nature; however, he had this child-like side that made me love him with every ounce of my entire being. Unfortunately, if we let Jake and Collin run wild with their plots and plans, there was a good chance this whole trip to Switzerland would be ruined, and everyone would be pissed off in the end.

"Listen up," I said. "I would like this trip to Switzerland to be spent with *you*, enjoying the festive season. Is there any chance this retaliation can wait until *after* the holidays?"

Jake studied my expression and smiled adoringly, "Baby, I would *never* ruin our Christmas. In fact, the way Collin and I plan to *repay* my brother for helping us focus on our wives and families this holiday season is to ensure this is a Christmas that none of us will ever forget."

"That's what worries me," I said with a laugh. "How about we do it this way? Tell me what you have planned, and I'll decide whether all of us will be victims in your and Collin's little schemes."

"If I told you, then it would ruin Christmas," he said, trying to shy away from revealing anything to me.

"It's going to ruin Christmas if you keep secrets from me," I said, standing my ground with my stubborn husband.

"Fine," he conceded like our son would when being scolded for upsetting his little sister. "But you won't believe me when I tell you."

"Try me," I said. "And trust me, all I've wanted this holiday season is you. *Us*. I've missed us and was willing to do anything to return to the days when it was just me and you. So long as I have my husband every night and wild and crazy sex to complement it, I'm sure I'll be fine with your plans."

"And that's exactly what the plans entail," he said, walking over to me and helping me up from my chair. "To ensure," his lips claimed my neck in a hungry way that instantly pulled me out of questioning wife mode and turned me on so much that he couldn't get me over to the bed fast enough, "that everything we do is to make sure our wives will never forget this Christmas." His warm breath tickled the base of my neck while his hands worked to remove my velvet lounge pants, "Then Jim and his *besties* will be forced to do all the festive activities, forcing them to close their laptops and not check their phones for the entire time we're here."

I inhaled sharply when Jake's fingers slid into my wet entrance, which was throbbing and aching for him, and I suddenly couldn't care less about the plans he and Collin had conjured.

I'd heard enough to know that Jim and his friends would be participating in holiday activities instead of being on their laptops, and that was good enough for me. The CEOs, who *never* left their laptops shut for a day, would be thrown into whatever Christmas revelry Jake and Collin could pull out of their asses, which meant we were about to be entertained for the holidays in a whole new way.

# CHAPTER 24

❄

Ash

M y heart was full, and my sexual appetite was satiated by the time we arrived at the massive cabin-style home where we were to spend our Christmas holiday. The train experience was unbelievable, and now, we were spoiled beyond words in the luxury of this home with the most magnificent views of the Swiss Alps.

"Well? What do you think so far?" Avery asked, peeking from around the other side of Jim.

I leaned into Jake, who had his arm lovingly around my waist, and smiled as if I was on my honeymoon. Jake and Jim—although I knew the brothers were ready to battle it out somehow after the Maldives incident—both seemed to lay their weapons down for the moment and indulge themselves in the serenity of the atmosphere surrounding the majestic home nestled perfectly in the hillside.

"I'm honestly at a loss for words at this point," I chuckled. "I mean, after being in the Maldives and now whisked away to Santa's dreamland, I don't think I could ask for a more charming, old-world start to Christmas."

Jake's arm squeezed me gently, allowing me to glance up at his handsome face to see a smile of adoration.

"Well, we haven't kicked off Christmas just yet, angel," he said, glancing over to Jim and then back to me. "Trust me, your holiday spirit is about to turn into something that the Hallmark Channel would be jealous of."

"Well," I said, smiling but feeling nagged about missing my kids and wishing they were experiencing all this.

"Well, what?" Avery asked.

"I don't know. I didn't want to say anything because I appreciate all this time alone with Jake and all of you. But—"

"You miss the children?" Jim spoke with a hint of humor.

"I just can't help it."

Jake chuckled. "You're a perfect wife, and the best mother our kids could ask for, baby," he said as we walked through the atrium, then turned me to face him. "And this is where your first Christmas wish comes true."

As if this part was rehearsed, our kids, my dad, and stepmom appeared from a side door.

The rest of our friends who had followed us were filtering in around us, their kids bouncing down the stairs, but all that faded when I saw John and Kaley with my dad and Carmen.

"Merry Christmas, babe," Avery said, holding onto her youngest daughter, Izzy, while their oldest daughter, Addy, gave Jim the biggest bear hug a daughter could offer her father. Jim had adopted Addy when she was five, and the amount of love and affection between them went as deep as their bond.

It was an enchanting, picture-perfect moment, and tears filled my eyes as I hugged my excited son and watched as Kaley leaped into her dad's arms.

"You flew our family out for this?" I finally asked Avery as Carmen and Dad showered us with hugs.

"We did. Merry Christmas, everyone!" Jim announced as if he'd just saved Christmas for everyone across the world.

"Merry Christmas, indeed," Jake said, clasping his hand on his brother's shoulder. "This is amazing, man. I'll give you that."

Jim turned while all the kids joined up and ran off through a side door as if they owned the place. "So? All is forgiven, then?" he said, rocking back on his heels and sliding his hands into his trouser pockets.

Jake chuckled, and in true-to-form fashion, his daring expression reappeared.

"The best part," Jake started while the group of friends gathered around, "is that you will never know, big brother, but I promise you this: you *will* find out."

"Jake," Nat interrupted, and she and Spencer joined us, "I think everyone should lay their differences aside and enjoy spending Christmas together in the most beautiful place—"

"Listen to you, Nat," Collin said, joining where the group was forming to find out whether Collin and Jake were going to relax and enjoy Christmas or screw with all the people who had a hand in their previous discomfort. "You never talk like this. One might believe you were prompted by your husband to encourage Jake and me to lay down our swords so all of you can sleep well every night we share this home."

I eyed Laney, rolling her eyes at her husband's taunts. If there were two people who knew our husbands would not let it end well, it was us.

"Ah," Jake said, seeing the group of CEOs eye each other with concern, "no one thought about that, did they? Sharing the home with me and Collin after you screwed with us in a practically inhumane way?"

"Jakey, Jakey," Alex said as his wife, Bree, chuckled at the men's exchange, practically setting themselves up to go to war right here and now. "Let's all just relax and enjoy the holidays. Bree and I are only here for the night. In the morning, we're heading to Austria to meet with an architect, and then we're going back home to the kids."

"Why are you two bailing out on this festive occasion? Austria is just a hop, skip, and a jump away?" Jake asked, a little bummed since all these guys were as close as brothers.

"We've been super fortunate to work with Lyle's Architect Firm, and I've been working for months on my drawings, hoping we could merge on an exciting project, which includes restoring castles and ruins. If all goes well, our firm will be known overseas," Bree excitedly answered.

"That's wonderful, Bree," I said. The woman had immense talent and skill when she was left to design and allow her passion for architecture to breathe through her. That's what was wonderful about her and Alex getting together. He took over the executive part of the business she carried on for her father so she could focus on what she really loved like she had before her father passed away. Getting this opportunity was a dream come true for my sweet friend.

"Yes," Nat said. "My fabulous bestie has finally hit it big, and it's about damn time the rest of the world gives her the recognition she deserves."

"Well, I'm not *that* big, but I love the castles, and being a part of this project would be my dream. If things go well, we may have the twins flown out to us, and we'll stay over here for the next month or so. It depends on how it shakes out," Bree said, smiling at her husband.

Seeing everyone happy and in love was enough for me to call it Christmas and leave it here. It would suck having Alex and Bree leave, but I knew we'd make the most of it. I'd have loved it if all our friends could've come, but I also knew how difficult it could be to pull off such trips around the holidays. Luckily, we usually managed to pull off some miracles and get together for New Year's Eve, which was always a highlight for me, but I wished we could've all been together in this magical place this Christmas.

"Looks like you found an easy way to get out of the shit you started," Jake said, pulling me out of my dreamy thoughts.

"Last I checked, I'm a brilliant man," Alex said, offering a cocky grin. "So, when I was afforded an opportunity to collaborate on a perfect prank against you two, knowing I would be leaving right after

I got to watch you find out about it, I didn't hesitate to be a part of it. The icing on the cake is that it worked out perfectly for Bree to spend time with the ladies for a bit before we rush off to Austria."

"And it *afforded you the opportunity* to wonder now how we will nail your ass after you get back from the lovely country," Collin said.

"Indeed," Alex said, too confidently.

"Let's go eat. I'm starved," Jim said. "I had the chefs prepare various dishes I'm sure everyone will enjoy. If we stay here and continue to talk, we'll keep the wheels turning in Jake and Collin's heads, and I'm not in the mood to deal with fake fire alarms every night until we leave," Jim smirked at Jake and then turned to guide us through the area where our kids had disappeared through.

The grand table was spread with a bounty of food. Candles were lit in their candelabras down the length of the long table, with silver chargers and crystal wine goblets at each place setting. A side table held a gingerbread village that looked like it was assembled by a team for a baking competition, alongside tiers of cookies and cakes. Big red ribbons and giant gold ball ornaments hung from the ceiling, and lights twinkled everywhere in the room.

"It looks like Jim called the White House holiday decorators and had this place turned into some magical Christmas land," Collin said with a laugh.

The kids were playing a board game on the floor next to a fireplace in the corner of the grand dining hall next to a decorated Christmas tree, which had to have been twenty feet tall.

Everyone remained quiet and awestruck by the opulent, festive dining hall. We were seated at the table while the staff filled our crystal wine glasses, and a different set of staff tended to our children. I would've felt bad about not spending more time with them since we arrived, but they seemed to forget we existed, so I thought it best to let them enjoy themselves for now.

Jim stood and raised his glass while the wait staff stood against the wall, waiting for any requests.

"It is my greatest honor to be able—"

"That's enough of that. You can sit," Jake said, standing from where we sat at the table across from Jim and Avery. "It is indeed an honor, and that is for sure," he said, smiling at Avery, who we all knew was responsible for the idea of spending Christmas together like this. "And you, Mrs. James Mitchell. You have indeed outdone yourself with all of this," he glanced around the great hall. "I'm speechless about all this—"

"This glorious and beautiful holiday décor?" Collin said to help Jake.

"Ah, yes," Jake said, smirking at Collin. "Thanks, man."

"It's nothing," Collin dramatically answered. "The ego-death has brought out a more appreciative side of me, you know?"

"I *do* know," Jake answered. "I feel it so deeply. All of this," he looked back at Jim, silently studying his brother's next move. "If it weren't for my big brother, helping me to see life through a different—"

"Lense?" Collin finished Jake's sentence while we remained silent, wanting to know where this would go.

"Lense, yes. It's like my outlook on everything is entirely different now. I feel connected to the earth and, dear God." He raised his hand, gesturing at the windows that spanned the walls behind where we sat. "Look at all of that. Majestic, inspiring, and so much more than I deserve."

"Here! Here!" Collin added.

*What the hell are they planning?* I thought, knowing this wasn't genuine. This was Jake getting ready to pull some crazy shit, and Collin knew what it was.

"All of that leads me to feel the Christmas spirit in a way I haven't since I was a young boy."

"The inner-boy thing?" Collin questioned Jake as if he didn't know where my husband was going with this.

"Yes. It took a shit-ton of shit leaving my system to find that inner boy of mine," Jake looked back at Jim.

"Well, get to it, then," Jim challenged. "What does your inner boy want to say, Jacob?"

"That we must celebrate this holiday the right way," Jake said.

"How the hell is *this* not the right way?" Spencer said while Nat continued to eye Jake skeptically.

"Simple. You know, while I was shitting in a hole I dug out in the woods," Jake looked at every man who had a hand in pranking him, "I learned that life is so much simpler and much more enjoyable when you create the memories yourself. When *you* work to make Christmas, miracles happen."

"I felt that, too," Collin said. "I think it happened when I was hand-digging my shit hole," he added so everyone would understand where he and Jake were coming from with this nonsense.

"All that said," Jake turned back to the wait staff, "we appreciate you and all the work that went into this amazing spread. However, we won't require your services any longer. You are *all* free to leave, paid in full for the time you have been scheduled to work." He looked at Jim's somber expression, "A Christmas present from the big man himself."

"What are you doing?" Jim asked, bored with Jake's gesture.

"I'm dismissing all the staff here to create a perfect Christmas for us men, who have been neglecting our beautiful wives and kids all year, to do everything ourselves."

"You're going to cook for everyone?" Jim said with an annoyed expression.

"No, my good brother," he eyed every man sitting at the table, "*We* are going to cook and bake and cut down our own Christmas tree, then watch the children so the women can indulge in shopping for Christmas goodies," he said in a silly tone and an excited shiver. "All the stuff we'd naturally *hire out*, we're doing ourselves."

"This is ridiculous," Jim said.

"This is a fantastic idea," Nat was the first lady to agree with Jake's plans.

"There she is," Collin cheered Nat, who was no longer on the side of the CEOs and was joining forces with Jake and Collin instead.

"It *is* a fantastic idea," Avery added. "Jim's an amazing cook, and he and Addy love baking together."

"And I think it would be an awesome memory for John to have, cutting down a Christmas tree with you." I smiled up at Jake, relieved that this was how he had chosen to get back at his brother and the rest of the men.

This could be fun.

"That's fair," Jim said. "Fine. We'll dismiss the staff and entertain our wives and children just like Jakey suggests," he agreed, but I could see the wheels spinning in Jim's head.

"Then, it's settled. Tomorrow, our spoiled asses will do everything ourselves until after Christmas day."

"And this is your cute little way of retaliation?" Alex chuckled.

"I'm not retaliating," Jake said. "I'm sharing a gentler, more peaceful way of viewing the holidays this year. When you live three to four days in deep meditation, learning how to ground yourself, you learn that a life lived simply and without all the spoils and riches of material possessions is a life well lived."

"And you'll find the sex much more remarkable, too," Collin said. "Because in everything we're about to do to share our holiday cheer, I'm confident Jim and Spencer will find their ego death. That, my friends, is where the amazing sex comes in," he finished with a smirk to Jake.

"It's a shame your handsome ass won't be here to enjoy it," Jake said, looking at Alex. "But once you see the better side of these bastards, you'll be begging us to teach you what we learned on the meditation retreat you all signed us up for."

"To the merriest Christmas of all," Jim said, not the least bit intimidated by Jake's unexpected announcement and takeover of the holidays.

"One that will make memories to last a lifetime," Jake answered.

# CHAPTER 25

❄

Jake

Collin and I were up before everyone in the house, getting our plans in motion.

"How many fireplaces did you count?" I asked. Collin had been working on a different part of our plan while I confirmed reservations for a place in the village square to rent and play out a live Nativity scene. It was something I'd seen in a Christmas comedy movie, and although they didn't have a designated place for live Nativity acting stuff, they *did* have locations that you could reserve in the outdoor market. After a brief conversation with the people who ran the place, I was able to reserve it for a night for a couple of hours so the guys could act out the Nativity scene, farm animals and all.

"There's one in every fucking room, so there's probably at least twelve," Collin said with a chuckle.

"Okay. We're confirmed for tonight for the Nativity, which is the perfect way to kick off all this shit."

"Excellent timing. It's as if the Universe was working on our behalf without us even having to try," Collin said.

"That's because we did so well during meditation hell week," I answered. "All right. The sun is about to rise, and I'm not about to let those dipfuckers sleep another second."

"Rise and shine, baby," Collin said, and then we were on our way up to wake up Spencer, Alex, and Jim.

"WHAT THE HELL ARE YOU DOING?" Jim grumbled, shielding his eyes from the lights I flipped on after entering his and Avery's room.

"Sorry, Avery," I acknowledged my sister-in-law after she almost threw something from her nightstand at me.

"Seriously, Jake?" Avery said. "Why the hell are you tormenting me while you torture your brother?"

"That's Jim's fault," I stated proudly. "If he would've taken me seriously last night when I told him I'd see him at sunrise, he would've known I would be in here to wake him up if he wasn't downstairs at 0500 hours."

Jim slid out of bed while Avery snuggled into the bed further, enjoying that she could now stretch out and utilize the entire bed for her comfort.

"When did you start using military time?" Jim said, pulling on a pair of sweats from the dresser drawer he'd packed his clothes into.

"Since I became a doctor and had to start calling times of death?" I returned.

"Don't be so morbid. It's Christmas," he said, trying to be funny.

I watched with humor as my brother, who prided himself on always being perfectly groomed, looked like a disheveled mess.

"You look like you lost a wrestling match to a silverback gorilla," I said. "We have no time for you to fix that bedhead situation you've got going on."

"Jim, just go with him," Avery said, unable to return to sleep so long as I was in here using my *outside voice*, ensuring that Jim got his ass kicked out of the room wearing his sweatpants and T-shirt.

The only thing he'd be changing into today would be some shepherd's clothing circa 2500 b.c. for tonight's Nativity. There was certainly a method to all this madness, and if Collin's game were rolling as tight as mine, Spencer would be in the same position as my brother. Whomever of us was first to get their CEO's cocky ass out of bed would claim the victorious prize of waking up Alex, which we didn't have much time to do since we only had a few hours before he was out of here and off to Austria with his wife.

"I'm trying to find—"

"No need for that," I said, grabbing Jim's arm and leading his half-awake self from the room.

"What the hell are you doing?" Jim growled.

"Jesus, your breath," I waved my hand in front of my face, then grinned. "That's *so* going to suck for you if we're too busy to stop, and you don't have time to brush your perfectly polished teeth!"

Jim smacked my hands away from where I pinched each side of his cheeks, provoking him.

"I will fucking knock you out," Jim warned.

I feigned horror as we walked down the dimly lit hallway, "And ruin Christmas? I highly doubt you'll do such a thing, you miserable old bear."

"Trust me, it won't ruin Christmas for anyone but you," Jim answered, annoyed.

I grinned, "When the kids hear that Uncle Jim knocked out their dad like we're a couple of teenagers, I think it will ruin Christmas for my family."

"How long is this going to go on?" Jim asked, turning to me and trying to stand tall and firm like the big bad CEO he naturally was.

I stared into his darkened emerald irises, "You're not nearly as uncomfortable as I was whilst shitting in a hole in the forest on the *first night* of that stupid little psycho meditation clinic you tricked my ass into attending. So, I'm not sure how long it will take to bring you to your knees while spreading holiday cheer."

He narrowed his eyes at me. "You're spreading something, but it isn't fucking holiday cheer," he said, rubbing his tired face.

"True. Now," I grabbed his arm again, making him jerk away like I knew he would. "First things first," I said, seeing that Collin already had Alex in his pajama bottoms and Spencer in a pair of jeans. "We need to get all these fireplaces lit, and get the house warmed up for that cozy cabin feel that the ladies boasted about so much last night."

"Are you fucking with me right now?" Alex asked as Jim and I reached where the men all stood, fucked-up hair and all, at the bottom of the steps.

"I was about to ask you the same thing, Grayson," I laughed, looking at the cartoon Santa Clauses printed all over his white and red fleece pants. "I see Mrs. Claus had her way with your ass last night?"

"And from what I deduced since this cutie pie fell out of bed wearing them, that's all the dipfucker got for Christmas last night," Collin added.

I grinned while the men chuckled, "I'm telling you, *ego death* translates to the best sex ever. You don't see my ass sleeping in Santa jammies, do you?"

"I only see your ass looking and sounding like fucking Buddy the Elf. You're annoying the shit out of me," Alex retorted.

"Nah, man," Collin said with a laugh. "He's not annoying at all. Look at Jim and Spence. They're not even annoyed by him, most likely because we all got laid last night instead of gifted Christmas jammies."

"If you must know, my wife enjoyed amazing shower sex—"

"Meh, no one wants to know about that, Alex, just about how you lost your balls and covered what was left of your dick with these cartoon pants of yours," I said, laughing.

"What are we doing?" Jim grumbled.

"You never were one for mornings," I said.

"Oh, did your inner boy just now recall that?" he answered.

"Let's get some coffee," Spencer interrupted. "Where's the goddamn espresso machine? This is the Asters' place, so I know they've got nothing but the finest—"

"Yeah, about that," Collin said. "We're not using any fancy shit."

Jim stopped and turned back from his mission toward the kitchen for coffee. "Then what exactly do you propose we use to make our coffee?"

I pointed toward the firepit outside that Collin and I had lit after we first woke up. "It's called a percolator," I said, looking at the three businessmen. "It works very similar to the fancy French Press your spoiled ass loves to make your coffee from."

"You're just going to have to clean it and rinse it. Jake and I already used it to make our morning brew," Collin added.

Unexpectedly, Jim grinned at me, "How the *fuck* do you plan on not ruining Christmas when my lovely wife wakes up and discovers she's going to have to sit outside and percolate coffee while she freezes her ass off every morning?"

"That's the thing, Jimbo," I said, smacking my brother purposefully too hard on his back. "She's not going to do any of that shit. *You are!*" I smiled at him and the other CEOs who'd officially begun the first round of punishment we had for them. "Again, first things first. Fires need to be lit. There are thirteen of them, and wood needs to be brought to each one." I pointed toward the woodshed, "The wood for the fireplaces is out there."

"Of course, if you three use your genius CEO brains, you'll pick one of you to make the ladies their coffee while the other two go and get the wood and start lighting fireplaces," Collin said, trying to be serious.

"And what the hell are you and Collin going to do, supervise? Because that's not part of the plan, my friend," Spencer said.

"Of course not," I answered. "We're going to start cooking breakfast so everyone can have breakfast in bed, including our cute little bugs, sleeping in their cozy little beds."

What could I say? This was already working out to be quite efficient and lovely. I loved being in control over these bastards, and I was happy they were too tired to figure out how to weasel out of this. The key to staying in control was keeping one step ahead of my brother.

# CHAPTER 26

❄

Ash

When I woke up, I had no idea where my husband was or when he'd gotten out of bed. Instead of hunting him down, I opted for a nice hot shower to prepare for the day ahead. Being in Jake's arms last night and reaching extraordinary levels of passion was enough for me not to question whatever he was planning to do to get the other men back. Having my husband ravish my body with a renewed sense of intensity in his sexual appetite left me feeling blissfully happy and loving our renewed energy.

Everything felt light and effervescent again, and it filled my heart with so much happiness that I honestly didn't even want a material gift for Christmas this year. I had everything I had been yearning for all year: my children were happy, and my husband was in my arms, taking an extended break from work and renewing his mind, body, and spirit.

"Ohhh…Jingle bells, Jimbo smells…" I heard Jake's excited voice singing as he came into the bedroom, "…Alex ran away…" he sang, smiling at me as I walked out of the bathroom, "...Spencer's pissed, and Collin's—" he stopped, setting a breakfast tray on the bed I'd made before getting into the shower. "Hmm, I can't think of a rhyme for that part. Oh, well."

I chuckled, walking over to him and wrapping my arms around his neck as he welcomed me into his warm embrace. "Why don't we keep to the regular lyrics?" I said, stepping back and eyeing his vibrant expression. "Well, you're in a *jolly* mood this morning, so either the sex was amazing last night, or you've already succeeded in paying your brother back?"

He kissed the tip of my nose. "Baby, I'm in this jolly mood because I know my wife is going to have the best Christmas she could ever ask for." He paused and smirked at me, "And my brother is working to make it all possible."

"What have you already done?" I questioned. "You know, if you piss that man and his friends off the entire time we're here, it's going to—"

"Look at the delicious breakfast I just brought you," he said, kissing my forehead, "made by Collin and me."

"The scrambled eggs look delicious," I said. "Now I know what you and Collin were up to this morning, creating a magnificent breakfast-in-bed experience. Thank you for that. Did Jim, Alex, and Spencer help?"

"You should know that by now. Was Jim bitching when he came in to light your fire?" he asked.

"I didn't see Jim come in the room. I was in the shower," I answered, looking at the fireplace. "I'm confused."

"Jim lit the fire. That was his job this morning since the staff aren't here." He took my hand and walked me over to sit on the sofa next to the fireplace. "Sit, angel," he said, acting like he was my servant as he walked over to the bed, grabbed the tray of food, and set it in my lap. "It was already announced last evening that the men will do everything on our own to ensure our wives are doted upon and spoiled this Christmas. We're always busy and never around, so to show all of you how much we appreciate what you do while we run off to work, we're going to take care of you in every way we can. It's a lesson for all of us, not just Jim, Spence, and Alex. We need to show our wives how much we appreciate what you do to give us a warm, loving home to come to every night."

I listened to the line of shit he was feeding me while I spread blackberry jam over my toast, "Perhaps Avery and Nat are falling for your cute, kiss-ass way of sucking up to us just so we don't stop you from torturing those guys, but I'm not buying any of this."

Jake knelt and took the poker to move the logs in the fireplace to create more flame. "You are definitely my wife," Jake chuckled, then looked back at me. "I can't get shit past you."

"No, you can't." I took a sip of coffee and immediately spit it back into the cup. "Jesus," I said, quickly taking a swig of orange juice to remove the bitterness from my taste buds.

"Too strong?" Jake asked, taking a sip. "Fucking hell, that's disgusting. Well, that's Alex's fault. I told him not to let the percolator boil the water, and he must've neglected to—"

"Hold the hell up," I said, looking at him in question. "Percolator? Are we suddenly camping on the frontier now? What happened to using a regular coffee maker?"

I smiled at Jake's devilish grin, which would've been handsome if it wasn't so worrisome at the moment. "We're not using one."

"Why not?"

"Collin and I believe that if we all go the extra mile to show we are willing—"

"Stop it with the bullshit, Jacob," I interrupted him. "What did you make Alex do? The poor guy has to fly to Austria today, and I know that—"

"Poor guy?" Jake stopped me. "Allow me to remind you that the *poor guy* of whom you speak hired an actor to give Collin and me *natural laxatives* so we'd shit our brains out all night long for two days in a row in holes that we dug with our hands."

I covered my smile because it was a pretty awful prank.

"You think it's hilarious," he pointed to my smile.

"No," I said, trying to be serious. "Listen to me, I thought the prank

THE HOLIDAYS WITH DR. MITCHELL 147

was harsh," I framed his handsome face with my hands and tenderly kissed his pouty lips, "but you don't need to punish these guys all week, and I know that's what you're planning."

"Who gives a shit if Alex was outside, freezing his ass off while waiting for coffee to perk?" he said. "He'll survive, and it's not inconveniencing any of you ladies. The rules are still being followed."

"The coffee tastes disgusting, though, and we all know how seriously Avery takes her coffee," I said, trying to warn Jake that their silly games would end up ruining things for the innocents.

"Well, she can blame Alex. Coffee isn't that fucking hard to make. He should've taken the small task he was given seriously." He pointed at the fire, "Jim seems to have successfully handled his first Christmas task well, don't you think?"

I nodded. "Seriously, though, Jake. You're skating on thin ice. Everyone is here to enjoy the holidays, and Jim and Avery have gone out of their way to make this enjoyable and memorable for everyone."

"Jim definitely went out of his way to make the Maldives memorable for *me*, so I merely want to ensure that he views Switzerland the same way I now view the Maldives?"

"That's how you're going to screw something up. You're not thinking clearly in your retaliation," I informed him. "In the Maldives, Laney and I were pleasantly pampered on that island of bliss while you two were being screwed with. The difference now is that you're planning to screw with them while we're all in the same home."

"Who gives a shit?" Jake said, almost upset that I was spoiling his plans. "I promise this will not affect any of you."

I studied my husband's youthful expression and knew it was eating him alive not to get back at his brother quickly and easily. Everything was slowed down because it was a family holiday, and the women and children could easily become innocent victims if he weren't careful.

"Listen, baby," Jake said, "I know you're concerned about some holiday fuckups happening, but what family out there doesn't have some drama over the holidays? Things go wrong when you're trying to make everything perfect. So, allow us to make it all wrong for those bastards who chose to fuck with us, then it will eventually go all right."

"That's the hill you're willing to die on if all this backfires in your face?"

"No one is dying on hills, and this isn't a war—"

"You made Alex sit outside and percolate coffee in the freezing cold like an old cowboy," I said.

"I promise you, angel," he said, running his hands excitedly up and down each side of my legs, which he'd been bracing while acting like a little boy begging his mom to go to the park and play. "You all will have a wonderful and *extremely* festive traditional and classic Christmas. It will be one that the kids will talk about for years to come, and in the end, we'll be laughing about it. Collin and I have planned this out very nicely, so allow us to pamper and spoil all of you with the best, most entertaining Christmas season you could ask for."

A moment later, the bedroom door opened, and I almost laughed when I saw that Jim and Spencer both looked like they'd just fallen out of bed and hadn't slept all night. That wasn't the concerning part, though. It was that, for the first time since I'd known the two extremely powerful executives, they didn't seem to care that they looked like they'd barely survived a buffalo stampede.

"Dear God, you both look like you haven't slept all night," I said, handing my tray of food to my husband.

"You don't say?" Jim said, forcing a smile on his face.

I couldn't help but laugh, seeing my brother-in-law in this shape. His hair was a disaster, and Spencer's was, too.

"Okay, well, do you guys need to shower?" I asked, unsure why they were in our room.

"Fuck!" Spencer said while Jim's eyes darkened and narrowed at his brother. "I forgot I haven't even taken a shower yet."

"There's no time for that," Jake said, waving them off, his eyes set on punishing these two men.

"Stop telling us what there is or isn't time for," Jim snapped. "I'm getting in the fucking shower and brushing my teeth. I'm just here to ensure you weren't trying to get laid while we were bringing in the last of the wood."

"Awesome," Jake said. "Now that's taken care of, we need to—"

"Jake," I said, interrupting him from treating Jim and Spencer like they were working on a chain gang. "Let them go freshen up."

Jim and Spencer smiled with their usual cockiness to Jake, igniting Jake's pettiness even more.

"There you have it. You don't want to upset your wife over the holidays by not listening to her, right?" Spencer asked.

"Of course I don't, and that's why you two need to help me and Collin harness the horses to the sleighs that the women will ride into town today."

Jim and Spencer's expressions of victory instantly faded when I gasped excitedly.

"That's right, baby," Jake said, walking over to me with a victorious expression. "Dress warm because I had two sleighs delivered this morning, and the horses to pull them should be here momentarily. I thought it would be thrilling for our wives to be pulled into town by sleigh since we're all in the North Pole spirit."

"The kids are going to lose their minds," I said. "I mean, wow."

"Wow is right," Jim said, his eyes laser focused on his little brother.

Jake snapped his fingers, "Chop, chop, Gentlemen. We have wives to indulge in Christmas cheers and fantasies."

Before I could say anything more, Jake led Jim and Spencer from the room to harness horses to the sleighs he'd rented. I had no idea how Jake and Collin had pulled this out of their hats so fast—to Jim and Spencer's extreme displeasure—but they had, and it was as comical now as it was entertaining. God only knew what else they'd planned, but if it stayed in the vein of elaborate Christmas traditions like horse and sleigh rides, we were guaranteed to have the most epic Christmas of all time.

# CHAPTER 27

❄

Jake

All right, all right. I let off the gas a little on my brother and his *partner in crime*, Spencer. Collin and I gave them enough time to freshen up and prepare for the newest round of Christmas madness —the *Live Nativity scene*, starring all of us.

"Where are the kids?" Avery asked us, even though we men weren't supposed to speak about anything unrelated to the Nativity.

I glanced at her where she stood in observance, bundled warmly in layers of scarves and a big, puffy coat.

"The Christ-child which you seek has been born," Collin declared as if he'd memorized the Nativity script for a play.

"You've got to be kidding me," my lovely and adorable wife said as she stood next to Avery and took in the visual of us dressed as the Three Wise Men and shepherds. "Where's Mary and the baby, though?" Ash questioned, looking around.

Unfortunately, I hadn't thought this part entirely through when planning to torture my brother by making him part of a live Nativity set. When Jim asked why we didn't have Mary or a baby in the manger, I couldn't understand his smug look when I said it would be fine without them. I knew I was doing this for all the wrong reasons, but I was banking on it turning out right in the end.

Regrettably, it seemed like the first visitors to our scene had noticed the plot hole I'd hoped would be overlooked, but what was I supposed to do, pull one of our wives up here to stand quietly as Mary and then recruit a baby? In *this* weather? I'd take my chances on screwing up the Nativity story over screwing with the wives.

Rules to follow, remember?

"Away in a manger…" Collin and I began responding in song.

That was another rule. If anyone questioned our Nativity story, our responses could only be returned by singing Christmas carols.

"Dad?" Addy questioned Jim, who was standing with his fake beard and wearing the purple robes of the Magi. "Who are you supposed to be?"

Jim remained solemn and as still as an authentic Nativity scene statue would.

"Answer your kid," Collin said, the second Magi in this scene, kneeling where Jim stood at his side. "In song, of course."

"No," Jim muttered back to him.

"You blow this and—"

"And what?" Spencer, the third costumed Magi, spoke.

"You'll ruin everything for our lovely wives," I said, proudly wearing the robes I imagined Joseph wore back in the day.

"I highly doubt that," Jim said.

"I think they're supposed to sing the answers," my sharp-as-a-tack wife said, catching on quickly.

"Ah, that makes sense. I just thought Collin and Jake were singing because they love to jump at the opportunity whenever it arises," Laney said, chuckling and playing along.

"That makes a lot of sense," Nat chimed in on cue. "So, that means Jim's got to answer Addy with a song like Collin and Jake did?"

"It's an interactive singing nativity," Avery said, chuckling and looking at Addy. "So, your dad's got to sing his answers to you."

I was doing everything I could to not laugh at this moment, which was working out so much more splendidly than I'd hoped to accomplish. When the ladies and the kids gained a vibrant sense of excitement for our nifty little Christmas play, the crowds gathered around. People looked inquisitively at us, speaking to each other in their native languages, primarily German, French, and Italian, with a sprinkling of British English here and there.

"Is it a musical?" an older woman with a thick German accent asked, realizing we had been speaking English and joining in.

"It's a nativity. I see that," her friend added. "But where's Mary and the baby?"

"Away in the manger…" I rang out with all my holiday cheer.

"But you're in a manger?" the first lady questioned while our wives and kids giggled.

"No crib for a bed…" Collin managed in his deepest baritone.

"Nice job, man," I complimented him.

"Well, this is adorable," a new visitor with a British accent said, walking up and smiling at the confusing scene where we sang interactively to our audience.

"What's cute is I think they've intentionally left out characters from the story in the hopes they would be questioned so they could sing back their answers."

"Wunderbar!" another lady said, looking like she'd dressed in a Christmas sweater she'd crafted from her crocheting skills. "I see Joseph," she smiled and pointed at me. "Now, how are those guys called again?" she pointed toward our three Magi men.

Collin stood from where he was kneeling and walked to stand in between Spence and Jim. "Together," Collin rang out in song, *"We Three Kings of—"* He paused and looked at Jim and Spence, who stood there looking like a couple of Grinches who stole this Christmas scene away from the crowd that was drawing in to be entertained by all of us.

"He's got a beautiful voice, Helga," our first visitor stated. "I don't understand why the other two won't sing."

"Maybe because they're afraid to?" Bless my wife for adding fuel to this fire.

"Oh, probably," Helga's friend answered Ash.

"My dad has a great voice," Addy said, the only child in tow because Carmen and Mark had taken the younger ones back home after the sun set and it got even more frigid. "Sing, Dad."

I couldn't resist looking at my brother, who was threatening to ruin all of this for his darling Addy because he was being a stubborn dickhead right now.

"Sing, asshole," I heard Collin whisper.

"Jim!" Avery snapped. "What the fuck are you doing?"

"*Mon Dieu!*" a woman behind Helga gasped, appalled by Avery's language at the foot of a Nativity scene.

"Oh my," another said. Now, Avery looked terrible because of her husband's stubbornness.

"I don't know where we are in the song," Jim grumbled *too loud*.

"Dad's going to ruin it," Addy said, looking at Avery in typical teenage-girl annoyance. "He's talking and not singing. I don't think he studied his parts."

"Me either," Avery said like Jim had had weeks to rehearse this Christmas family tradition, and he'd let the entire family down.

"*Star of Wonder, Star of Night...*"

"Is he drunk?" a random person questioned with a laugh.

Addy looked at Jim as if she half-believed the man's humored question, and I was doing everything I could not to laugh out loud. As much as I enjoyed Jim's discomfort, the one thing I didn't want to do was *mock* Christmas traditions for anyone, especially when I was unsure how seriously people took their nativity scenes on this side of the world.

Jim's irritation with me and everything he was exposed to was about to derail the whole thing, so it was time I saved him and saved Christmas and turned this all around.

I stood up and eyed Collin, giving him a look to let him know we had to bail the big guys out. So, that's when we took it from the top as if it'd all been planned this way. We sang *We Three Kings of Orient Are*, and I encouraged everyone who was confused and humored by our live Nativity to join in, and that's when the Christmas cheer kicked into high gear.

Everything had turned out for the best, and this was just the beginning. We still had planned legit caroling through the picturesque villages and down through this marketplace like characters out of Charles Dickens's *Scrooge*, followed by baking Christmas cookies with all the kids. Then, once we arrived at Christmas Eve, we'd follow the Swiss tradition of getting our tree at a local farmer's land—picked out by John, of course—and by the time Christmas morning rolled around, I suspected that our retaliation for the meditation chaos would be complete.

After the way tonight had worked out, we were practically there already. The only problem left to solve was Spencer, who seemed utterly unscathed by all of this. I suppose that meant he'd have to be the one to help John cut down the tree with a handsaw, which would be no easy task, given the size of the tree we'd need to fill the living room.

We were still a few days from crossing that bridge, so I hoped Spence would break for his benefit; however, at this rate, it seemed unlikely. Time would tell.

# CHAPTER 28

❄

Jake

*Christmas Eve Morning*

G reat sex, excellent family time, and inflicting torture on my brother and Spence had lifted my spirits through the roof. The grand finale was drawing nigh, and when all was said and done, I was confident that none of those cocky CEO sons of bitches would dare prank Collin and me again.

"So, what's on the agenda for today?" Ash's dad asked in humor.

I smiled at my father-in-law and took great pride in the fact that the man was entertained at Spencer and Jim's expense. Of course, Collin and I were suffering right alongside those bastards, but seeing Jim and Spence so far out of their comfort zones, going through withdrawals from being on their laptops and phones all damn day, made all these nonstop Christmas festivities downright enjoyable.

"Ah, yes. Today," I said, standing from the breakfast table and smiling at Jim and Spencer's bedheads. We'd worn their asses out yesterday chopping up firewood.

"Spit it out," Spencer said, his once ambivalent mood finally matching Jim's annoyance. "What Christmas song are we *honoring* by playing a festive Christmas event for *the ladies and children?*"

"Excuse me?" Nat snapped, staring at her husband. "What the hell was that?"

"It's nothing," Spencer grumbled, and my lips were pressed into a fine line, trying not to laugh.

"The hell it isn't," she said. "You're lucky our daughter didn't hear that or the fact that you won't be getting laid tonight for daring to refer to the children and women in such an annoyed tone."

"I thought you were excited to keep up these festivities after seeing the look on your daughter's face yesterday when you helped her make *Lady Winter* the snowwoman?" Collin questioned, provoking Spencer even more.

"Precisely," Nat said. "This sour mood you're in is beyond me."

"Beyond *you?*" Spencer said, too exhausted to be wise enough not to talk back to his wife. "Try having your ass jerked out of bed every morning by these two dumbasses *in the name of Christmas cheer—*"

"Spence, stop," Jim tried to warn Spence from continuing down this paved road to hell. "You've enjoyed this."

"Speak for yourself, Jim," Spencer said. "I think this has gone far enough. I've already put my email responses to auto-vacation mode, or whatever you call it. See, I don't even know what it's called because I never use it. And because I've chosen to ghost all our clients and partners, God knows how many deals we're losing while we prance around in homemade ugly Christmas sweaters, bake Christmas cookies, percolate fucking coffee outside, and—"

Either Nat punched the man in his balls, or the lights came on, and he'd realized what an asshole he sounded like. This could be bad for Spencer because what the ladies weren't seeing was the constant poking of these two bears that Collin and I had been doing behind the scenes to make ourselves feel better about the torture we'd suffered.

"Okay, okay. That's enough from Papa Bear," I said. "Nat, cut the old man some slack. He's tired. Fortunately, this will be his last big event, and he can sleep in tomorrow."

"Sleep in tomorrow? Tomorrow is Christmas morning, dipshit," Spencer snapped.

"Oh, shit. That's right," I eyed Collin with a grin. "Well, that sucks. Now, we should review today's itinerary before Nat divorces Spencer and takes everything in the marriage. Allow me to go over the plans."

"Hopefully, those plans consist of all you miserable shits leaving this house. I'm done with this thundercloud who thinks work is more important than spoiling his family during the holidays," Nat said.

"Do you see what you've caused?" Spencer asked. The poor guy honestly looked half awake and completely exhausted.

Which was the point.

"I haven't caused jack shit," I defended myself. "You're the one cracking under Christmas pressure, and if you keep this shit up, dialing *down* the Christmas spirit in this home, then Collin and I are sure to send everyone on a festive journey to the tune of the twelve days of Christmas. We haven't done anything from that song yet."

"It would be ideal if we could put together a little *Silent Night* event, if you ask me," Jim added.

"Well, no one is asking you, Jimmy," Collin said. "Don't try to co-sign on mine and Jake's ideas. Even though we found a crack in Spence, we're staying the course. Today, the reindeer arrive."

"Dear God," Ash finally said with a chuckle. I was surprised that she and Avery hadn't entered this conversation until now. "I can't even imagine what you guys managed with the *Rudolf the Red-Nosed Reindeer* song."

"No, my love," I said. "This was Collin's idea, and it's not about Rudolf. It's based on a little tune called *Grandma Got Run Over by a Reindeer.*"

"Oh?" Carmen said, coming in from the kitchen. "I'm the only grandma here, so I prefer we skip that event, eh? Abuelita ain't getting run over by *nada*!"

Everyone laughed except Spencer, who was more concerned about having pissed off his wife than he was entertaining another long day of Christmas chores.

"Don't worry, Carm. No abuelas will be harmed in the reenactment of this reindeer song," I assured her. "However, we will be using reindeer to pull our sleighs to Gersbach's farm in order to sail out over their acreage and find the perfect Christmas tree for the kids to hang the hand-crafted ornaments we made together the other day."

"What does that have to do with the song?" Avery questioned.

"Aside from the presence of reindeer, absolutely nothing, actually," Collin said. "Hey Jake, I know you wanted the reindeer and all, but we got to take this in a different song direction, or it won't work."

"Oh?" Jim perked up. "Our two Christmas elves have found themselves backed into a corner. Looks like we can't go in a sleigh to get the family Christmas tree."

I eyed my brother, "You could only dream of a day when Collin and I back ourselves into a corner, unable to continue what we started."

"*Oh, Christmas Tree*, duh?" Collin said. "How lovely are thy branches…"

He finished in song.

I grinned. "See, we're back on track. So, that's taken care of. Mark, do you want to come along with us?" I asked Ash's dad. "John's excited about this one, and I know your grandson would love to have you with us."

"Absolutely," Mark said.

"As for you ladies," I said, smiling at the women, "we've taken into account that this has been a long week of decorating, putting lights on the house, winning neighborhood Christmas competitions—"

"We're the only house on the mountain," Avery laughed. "You guys *did* do a fantastic job, though. It's beautiful."

"Indeed," I continued. "Anyway, we reconnected the main room's television."

"Skip to the point," Jim said. "I don't want another lecture about how technology was ruining our holidays."

"Well, the TVs are coming back into play, and you'll be glad to know I called the staff in again to help prepare meals while we're out today finding the perfect family Christmas tree."

"We did the Clark Griswold shit with the lights and house decorations last night, dude," Spencer said. "Let's just get a goddamn tree from a lot. We don't want any squirrels ruining the Asters' furniture."

"Ah, ah, ah," Collin waved his index finger at Spencer. "This has nothing to do with that movie. This has everything to do with following Swiss traditions and honoring how they celebrate as we show gratitude and appreciation for spending the perfect family Christmas in their country."

"By chopping down *and killing* one of their trees?" Spencer taunted.

"I'm not going down that road with you," I answered. "Nice try, though. In respecting Swiss traditions, we're going to harness some reindeer to a sleigh and have them bring us to a Christmas tree farm where we'll find and cut down our very own Christmas tree."

"That sounds exciting," Avery said.

"And bitterly cold," Nat added. "But Spencer could stand to do a little manual labor right now."

Spencer tightened his lips, realizing he should've never talked back so harshly to his wife.

"Nat, Spence was doing manual labor yesterday as well. He's the one who did the roof lighting and cut half a cord of wood," Jim said, coming to his defense.

"It really is cute watching you defend Spence as if he were your boyfriend," I taunted.

"Unfortunately, you all were at the market in the city center, unable to witness his efforts," Jim finished, ignoring me.

She looked at Spencer, "Is this true?"

"Yeah, and hey, I'm sorry for what I said. I'm just sore as hell, exhausted, and not in the mood to hear Jake's fucking chipper mouth through another *fucking Christmas song.*"

"Listen to me, baby," she said, disregarding everyone in the room and capturing Spencer's lips in a sensual kiss.

"Oh, come on, Nat," I said.

"Chill out, Jacob," she said, annoyed. "Now," she returned her attention to Spencer, "because you were a dick, you're still going on this reindeer adventure, but because you apologized and busted your ass for us with the Christmas lights and wood, you'll get a special little surprise tonight. You know, the one I vowed to take away from you moments ago?"

"Yeah?" Spence said with the broadest smile any man has ever managed. I rolled my eyes, seeing the bastard get off too easily.

"All right, pervs. Let's go," I said. "Get your parkas because it's going to be cold as shit out there." I looked around the table, "Ladies, enjoy your relaxing afternoon. The staff will be here to wait on you, and we'll be back before sundown."

If only I knew how haunting those words would be to me two hours into our Christmas tree hunt, I would've smartly grabbed at least *one* cell phone to ensure we wouldn't become stranded in the middle of nowhere...

# CHAPTER 29

❄

Jake

The reindeer were trained for pulling sleighs, and we were ready to get on our way after we got them harnessed to ours. All of us guys, Mark and John included, piled into the bright red Santa sleigh, and we set off to the Gersbach family Christmas tree farm to hunt for the perfect Christmas tree to cut down.

We were reenacting *Over the River and Through the Woods*, and honestly, it was cold as fuck out here; however, as with everything else we'd planned to the tune of a Christmas song, my discomfort was easily overlooked because of the discomfort my brother and Spence were experiencing.

The highlight was that my father-in-law and son were in spectacular spirits, which was driving my chipper mood—that and the fact that it was Christmas Eve, after all.

Collin and I sat in the front with John between us, and I had to hand it to Collin: he was pretty impressive in his skills for guiding reindeer. He maneuvered this rig like he was back home driving his

Lamborghini. It did help that the man grew up around horses as a kid, so I supposed that must've transferred to his knowledge about directing a six-reindeer sleigh. He also sat with the reindeer handlers for a solid few hours, getting tips on how to do this, so I couldn't give him *too* much credit.

"How deep into this forest are we going?" Jim questioned as Collin held the reins and guided the reindeer deeper into the woods.

"Until we find the perfect tree, Jimmy," I turned back and cheerfully proclaimed to my brother.

I smirked at Jim, Spencer, and Mark, all bundled up like snow bunnies, wearing beanies, scarves, and mittens, all crammed into the second row of the sleigh, trying to keep warm.

"I'm freezing my balls off," Spencer complained.

"There's hot cocoa that Mom packed, Uncle Spence," John answered.

I ruffled the top of John's beanie, finding happiness by seeing how exciting this was for him.

"And once we get this enormous tree, which you two will no doubt demand we cut down, how exactly do you plan on getting it back to the house?" Jim challenged, wholly unamused by our endeavor.

"We'll tie it to the sleigh and pull it back to the house like they did back in the day," I confidently returned.

"Don't you think that the poor reindeer will be pushed to their limits, dragging five and a half men and a tree through the snow all the way back to the house?" Spencer asked, trying to catch us fucking something up.

"That's what they have the tarp for," my father-in-law stated.

"Tarp?" Jim asked, taking his arrogant tone down a notch since he was speaking to Ash's dad, who was currently as jolly as Old Saint Nick.

"Yeah. When the boys asked me how we could get the tree back to the house, I mentioned that if we wrap it in a tarp, it will help it slide smoothly over the snow," Mark proudly proclaimed.

"So, you knew about this, Mark?" Spencer added.

"He found out the same time you two did," Collin said, cracking the reins like Santa, leading the sleigh through the starry night sky on Christmas Eve. "We just hadn't worked out that detail until right before we left. When Jake and I discussed it, Mark offered invaluable advice."

"And I said it would be too heavy for the reindeer," John added.

"Yeah, you did," I smiled down at my son. "Hey, Collin, why don't we let this kid take the reins for a minute or two?"

"Why the hell not?" Collin agreed. "Now, hold tight to the reins. You don't want to lose them, or we'll really be in trouble," he advised my giddy son.

"How do I make them go faster?" John questioned like a chip off the old block when it came to cranking up the speed.

"We're at a decent speed. If we go any faster, we'll be too cold to cut down a tree," Uncle Jim said from the back seat, trying not to be a dick but being a dick, nonetheless.

"I'm nice and toasty," I said, knowing the faster the sleigh went as it cut smoothly through the snowy forest, the more uncomfortable my brother and Spence would be. "You okay with going a little faster, Grandpa?" I glanced back at Mark, not wanting to subject an innocent man to the bullshit I was happily putting my brother and Spence through.

"I'm great. This is a hoot," Mark chuckled.

"Then, let's get these reindeer in another gear," Collin said, smiling at me and knowing that Jim and Spence were probably ready to murder us in our sleep. "Just give the reins a little smack. You don't want to hurt them; you just need to tell them you want a little more," he instructed John while placing his hand around John's shoulder to keep him focused and steady.

"Christ almighty," Jim grumbled when John snapped the reins softly, and the reindeer jolted into a faster prance.

"Shall we sing a carol?" Collin asked, knowing it would antagonize the living hell out of Jim and Spencer.

"*Dashing through the snow...*" John busted out in an excited laugh.

"*In a one-horse open sleigh...*" I laughed, not feeling so amused by the simplicity of life for too long.

I hadn't thought about work, surgeries, or science all week. I'd been fully immersed in my plans to torture Jim and Spencer, and because I'd planned a Christmas-themed revenge plot, I was focused on the holiday more than I'd ever been.

Bringing in all these traditions and making everything we did relate to a Christmas song made this time memorable. I was almost glad my brother and his idiot buddies tried their hand at fucking with me and Collin. Because of their antics, I'd inadvertently become the King of Christmas, and I was thoroughly happy with that.

"Oh no," John said when the sleigh unexpectedly dipped to one side while the reindeer continued at their fast pace.

"Here," Collin said, taking the reins to stop them.

The sleigh dipped harder on my side, forcing me to grab the wooden rail to keep from falling out. Once Collin managed to stop the reindeer, we got out to check out the sleigh and quickly realized the snow went up to our knees.

"Snowshoes would've been something—"

"Relax, Jim," I stopped his griping. "They're behind you. I just didn't think to strap them on before getting out to find out what happened." I reached my hand up to him, "Give me a pair. They're in that open area behind your seat."

"Meh, I don't know," Jim said, eyeing me humorously. "Having you buried to your waist in the snow is something I find rather gratifying at the moment."

"This is a sight I've been waiting to see all week," Spence humorously added.

While Jim and Spence took joy in my predicament, Collin, Mark, and my son got the snowshoes from the back and placed them on to assess what happened with the sleigh.

"Goddammit. It looks like the runner broke loose," Collin said.

"How did that happen?" I questioned, virtually stuck to my waist in the snow. "John wasn't going that fast."

"Well, we weren't driving the sleigh on packed snow," Mark offered. "So, it's more of a chore for the reindeer."

"Nice," Spencer said. "Not only did you dipshits bring us out in unpacked snow, but you also made it more difficult for the poor reindeer."

"Nice try, wise-ass," I answered, still waiting for one of the assholes to give in and get me a set of damn snowshoes. "Reindeer are literally made for this shit."

"Why because Santa uses them?" Jim mocked.

"Because their trainer told me so, dickwad," I said. "These guys can pull up to three hundred pounds at an average speed of eight miles per hour. A single reindeer has been—"

"Whatever," Jim cut me off. "I don't need a lecture on reindeer facts. What I want to know is how we're going to fix this problem while we're stuck in the middle of nowhere?"

"It's not going to be an easy fix," Mark informed us. "We need to find a way to reattach the runner to the body of the sleigh, and from what I see, it's going to need welding."

"Fresh out of welding torches," Collin said with a chuckle.

"Who's got a phone?" Jim questioned.

This was when I knew Collin and I had bitten off more than we could chew.

"Yeah, about that..."

"Jacob?" my brother said in a commanding tone so deep that he sounded like our father.

"*James?*" I returned because, quite honestly, I had nothing else.

"Are you both going to sit here throwing around your government names, or are we going to devise a plan?" Mark questioned.

"The plan is this," Collin said, looking back through the forest where there was nothing but our sled trail, which disappeared over the hillside we'd just come over. "Um—"

"Nothing like being broke down in the middle of the Alps on Christmas Eve with no one knowing where we are, and since both of you fuck-nuts have insisted we ditch our technology, we have no way to call for help," Spencer added in a voice that matched Jim's.

"What Christmas song do you boys have for us on this one?" Mark said, trying to douse the flames.

"I'll be home for Christmas comes to my mind immediately," Collin said, unaffected by our current state.

"Try again," Jim smarted off. "Due to this unexpected turn of events, we most certainly will not be home for Christmas. Is there a song for that? Something about smartasses who get everyone stranded in the snow in the middle of nowhere with no rescue in sight?"

"Well, you wanted Jake and Collin to bring in Silent Night," Mark chuckled at this inconvenient situation. "It looks like that's about to become a reality."

"That is very true," Spencer added with a laugh.

Of course, Spencer wasn't finding any of this humorous. His laugh was about Collin and me fucking up. Because of our hunger for revenge, Collin and I were responsible for being lost and stuck out here on Christmas Eve instead of happily bringing home the perfect Christmas tree in jolly spirits.

Goddammit. Why didn't I just bring my fucking phone?

# CHAPTER 30

❄

Ash

"My favorite Christmas movie is the *original* Miracle on 34th Street," I said, nestling into the fluffy blanket that Jake purchased for me as an early present at the Christmas market.

"Hmm. I thought you'd like the new one better—well, *new?* It's not exactly new if it's made in the 90s, eh?" Carmen said with a chuckle.

"Which is your favorite Christmas movie, Carm?" Nat asked.

"That's a tough one," she sighed. Kaley was fast asleep and curled into her by the chair next to the fireplace, "I'm not really into Christmas movies like that."

"Try," Laney said, chuckling.

"I always enjoy watching Christmas Vacation," she laughed. "There's something about Eddie and Catherine and that motor home that I find downright sexy," she teased, humoring us as we lounged around, enjoying our Christmas coziness.

"I love Little Women," Laney said, bringing up her all-time favorite book and movie. "The one with Winona Ryder. Maybe it's not *technically* a Christmas movie, but it's one of those movies I wouldn't watch if it weren't Christmas time."

"How cute. The book that brought you and Collin closer together," Avery chuckled.

"What about you, Av?" Nat asked, placing a candied almond delicately in her mouth.

"I'm sort of with Carm on this one. I'm not that into Christmas shows. If I *had* to think of one that puts me in the Christmas spirit every year, it's Rudolf the Red-nosed Reindeer. When I was broke, and my sister helped keep a roof over Addy's and my heads, we'd watch it together on TV, and Addy would squeal every time his nose lit up. Seeing my baby so happy on Christmas, even when I didn't have much to give her, was all that mattered, and that show always seemed to do the trick."

"It's still my favorite," Addy said, half-listening to our conversation while playing a card game on the floor with her little sister, Izzy.

"Is your sister still not talking to you?" I asked Avery, knowing the two had a falling out soon after she and Jim started dating.

"I have no idea what happened to her," Avery said. "We started talking a little before the holidays last year, but then she fell off the face of the earth again."

"Did you ever find out what her deal was?" Laney questioned.

"I don't want to dampen the holiday spirit too much, but I just saw my sister for who and what she is. She only was there for me because it put me in a position to depend on her. Once my life and situation got better, she wanted nothing to do with me. Honestly, she gets that from my mother. She only wanted to be in my life if she could manipulate it," Avery shrugged. "Anyway, let's change the subject. Those crazy guys put a lot of effort into us having a holly, jolly Christmas, and disappointing family members have no business ruining it."

"Speaking of the men who insisted we have the best Christmas ever," Nat said. "Where the hell are they?"

"Think about it," I said with a laugh. "Jake and Collin are going to put all of them through hell, trying to find the best tree in the forest.

I'm fairly confident they'll arrive as soon as the sun sets so it's dark, cold, and highly miserable out there to haul a Christmas tree into the house."

"They're probably holding hands and singing around the chosen holiday tree," Carmen said with a laugh. "Although if my honey bunny and grandson are cold, I'll kick all their asses."

"It *is* getting late," I said, growing more concerned after checking the time. "What if they got into some trouble?"

"They have cell phones," Nat said. "And after Spencer's attitude this morning, I'm quite confident he's chomping at the bit to use his and would use any excuse to do so."

"All I know is that we still have to decorate the damn tree, read *'Twas the Night Before Christmas*, and get these kids settled into bed before Santa harnesses up the true North Pole reindeer and heads our way," I said.

"I'm going to check on what's being made for Christmas Eve dinner," Carmen said. "I'm starving."

"The more I think about it, the more something doesn't feel right," I said, feeling uneasy.

"I think Jim and Spencer have been crying about that all week," Nat said. "Don't worry about the guys. Between the two brilliant business tycoons and two genius doctors, they'll be all right."

"That's what I'm worried about," I advised Nat. "Those two *doctors* act like foolish teenage boys sometimes."

"And those foolish teenage boys," Laney added, "have had Jim and Spence at their mercy all week."

"In the name of fully immersing themselves into the Christmas spirit for us," Avery added. "Jim knows his brother well, and he always has a backup plan in the event Jake screws something up."

"True," I acknowledged. "I'm just surprised they've been gone all day and haven't returned with a tree yet. It's just a Christmas tree."

"At the rate Jake and Collin have been riding my husband and Jim's asses all week on Christmas crack, I bet they're making them ride in that cold weather to various Christmas farms all over this mountainside to ensure their final night of retribution makes a big impact."

"Yeah, you guys are right," I conceded, knowing those scenarios were far more likely than anything terrible happening. "Let's see if the food is ready. Watching Christmas films all day has made me work up an appetite."

I walked over to the chair where Carmen had nestled Kaley and gently roused her.

"Hey, beautiful." I gently caressed my daughter's rosy cheek. "If you don't wake up now, you won't be able to sleep tonight, and Santa will skip our house," I said with wide excited eyes.

"Oh no," she grumbled, trying to ignore me and return to her cozy nap.

"Someone's in a nice and toasty Christmas Eve coma," I laughed. "Come here, honey," I reached to help her up. "Daddy's going to be back soon with John and Papa, and we need to be awake when they get home to see the perfect Christmas tree they got for us to decorate tonight."

"Okay," she agreed, half-smiling and wrapping her arms around my neck so I could pick her up.

"Let's see what we can find to eat in the kitchen, eh?"

We all took our lazy afternoon butts into the kitchen, and when the fragrance of the fondue foods being prepared for us to enjoy for dinner filled my senses, I practically drooled. From the look and smell of the various breads, vegetables, meats, and seafood being arranged on platters, I was going to be so full that I wouldn't be able to move by the time I devoured this delicious meal.

# CHAPTER 31

❄

Jake

"So, what's the backup plan?" I looked back at my brother, who sat huddled with Mark and Spence in the lopsided sled, trying to stay warm.

"You're honestly asking me that question?" Jim asked through gritted teeth.

"Yeah. You always have something in the back of your head to bail us out of any silly situation I might get us into."

"Silly?" Spencer grumbled. "You see this as *silly*?"

"Yeah, we're in a pretty fucked-up predicament right now," Collin acknowledged with a cringe.

"And Jim always pulls through with shit like this. There's no way you don't have a fucking backup phone on you."

"Guess again, fucker," Jim said. "No, I don't, or else I would've used it an hour ago to bail your delightful and full-of-Christmas-spirit ass out of this situation."

"I would've insisted Jake stays here while we warm up in the Asters' steam room," Mark said.

Now, I'd done it. I'd officially let down my once proud father-in-law.

Well, shit.

"We need to conjure an idea," Spencer said.

"I imagine the ladies will send someone to find us," Mark said. "Ash tends to worry more than Carmen, so I know she's got to be concerned now that the sun is setting."

"You'd think," Jim said. "However, don't forget the two nutcrackers who have created this entire festive week for everyone to marvel at. The ladies aren't worried at all. They know that Jake and Collin have been catering to them, making all their Christmas dreams come true while putting us through hell."

"No shit," I admitted. "They probably think we're keeping you out here purposefully."

"Since you created this madness, and Jimbo doesn't have your bailout backup plan," Spencer snapped, "what the fuck do you plan on doing to get us out of this situation?"

"Well," Collin said, eyeing me in a way to remind me that we never gave up and never surrendered, "we reach down, grab our balls, strap on the snowshoes, and lead the reindeer out of here in the direction we came."

"Brilliant!" I cheered, then looked at Jim. "You see, we don't just save lives through surgery; we save lives by thinking."

"Thinking?" Jim answered. "It would've been nice if that was something you were doing *before* we rode a damn sleigh who knows how many miles into a forest."

"Yeah, well, I'm *thinking* now, and that's what's saving lives. So, while I'm thinking," I said, scrambling out of this situation I'd fucked us into, "let's get a move on it before we get any colder and before it gets any darker."

"Just so I'm clear," Jim said, "in all your *thinking*, have you thought of how we're supposed to see out here while we walk through a dark forest *after* the sun sets?"

"The light of the moon, of course," Collin said cheerfully and back in action.

"You two aren't the geniuses you believe yourselves to be. You know that, right? I have no clue how you two ended up at the top of your fields," Spencer questioned with irritation.

"Keep your smug businessman insults to yourself, and let us *brilliant, life-saving doctors* save your asses, eh?" I answered, feeling confident we'd return in time for Christmas Eve.

Hopefully, we'd get there before our lovebugs went to bed, but at this point, the important part was making it back without frostbite.

"And what if Mark's heart gives out?" Jim smarted off.

"Fat chance," I said, looking at Mark. "I fixed that ticker so well that it probably works better than ours. Don't let my brother put that nonsense in your head."

"True that," Collin said, eyeing Jim. "It's *you* who should worry about heart failure after growing so comfortable accommodating Addy's every McDonald's whim."

"Are we going to sit here all night while the sun races down the other side of that mountain, or are we going to get the hell out of here?" Mark questioned.

"Hey, Dad," John said. "Do you think we can ride the reindeer?"

"Those guys aren't made for that, buddy," I said. "It would be nice if they were, though."

"Another hole in your game revealed," Jim said as we all began strapping on our snowshoes.

I wasn't going down like this. I wasn't going to crash and burn on my own game that was going so fucking well up until the sled cracked under pressure. No way in hell was that happening. So, I pressed forward and spun this into a tale that would make everyone believe this was the plan all along.

"That's the best part," I said while we all went to work unharnessing the reindeer from the sleigh. "This was all part of the plan."

"Oh, for fuck's sake," Spencer said. "Try again, Jakey."

"I'm serious. We shook all of you up, thinking we were stuck out here. The ladies will soon be saddened that we haven't returned in time for Christmas, and while they think they're going to have a *Blue Christmas...*" I sang as Collin looked over at me and grinned, "that's when everyone will see us walking up that snow-plowed driveway, singing *I'll be Home for Christmas.*"

Jim stared blankly at both me and Collin and sighed, "Do you even realize how fucking cheesy all of this is?"

"Cheesy, as in the most ridiculous bullshit you've ever been through?" I cockily returned, guiding my deer by the reins and helping John with his as we all began walking the way we came.

"Yes. I may never sing another Christmas song again because of how stupid this has been," Jim said.

"There's our Grinch," Mark chuckled. I loved this man for not getting pissy about this bullshit when he had every right to.

"Uncle Jim, you know Dad is just a big goofball," John said, trying to ease Jim out of his cranky mood.

"This is true," Jim smiled down at my son. "Let me ask you something, John?"

"Sure," my son answered, unfazed by what we were going through.

"Are you having a good time? A *Merry* Christmas?"

I watched the amused expressions of Spencer and Mark, looking at John for his answer.

"I am. All I usually ever think about at Christmas time is getting presents, but this whole week, I haven't even thought about them."

"Well," I said, my eyes widening in humor, "if anything makes all this worth it, it's that statement."

"That doesn't mean I don't want any presents, Dad," John insisted.

"Then what does it mean?" I questioned.

"It means this week has been so much fun. Even doing this," he reached up to hold his grandpa's hand, "I'll never forget this as long as I live."

"That's a lot of years you'll be thanking your dad for nearly killing all of us," Spencer said with a laugh. "You'll definitely never forget it if your toes freeze off."

"Mom made sure I wore thick socks, and I've got a bunch of layers under my winter coat. I'm actually sweating a little bit," John giggled like an eight-year-old, dropping his usual forty-year-old demeanor. "Seriously, Dad. This is so much fun. Everything has been."

"Does it make up for me missing your band recital at Thanksgiving?" I asked.

John rolled his eyes. "I was never upset about that; that was Mom."

"That's good to know, but it makes me sad that your mother was upset," I answered truthfully.

"I think she's better now," John grinned at me.

"I'm glad this has given you good memories," Jim said before smiling at me with approval.

From the look in Jim's eye and the change in his demeanor, I could tell things had become clear to him. Jim and I were raised in a wealthy family, but our family had detrimental problems and gave us issues that nearly cost us our happiness. Our mother was a drug abuser and alcoholic who was never present even on Christmas, and our father was a broken-hearted man who spent his days buried in work to escape the harsh reality of feeling unlovable. My father had amassed a fortune but sacrificed all his relationships to get it, leaving himself isolated and unhappy.

Somewhere down the road, Jim and I started to see life differently. I'd like to say it was before we met our wives, but it was after nearly losing them that we worked to keep our heads out of our assess and appreciate everything in life that we were blessed with that money could not buy.

I was relieved my son didn't rely on our wealth to make him happy. I loved that, at this age, he was experiencing that true happiness came from being around those you loved—even if it meant walking down some isolated path in the middle of the forest.

This was what it was all about, being together, doing stupid shit, and having fun. The most important thing was that we were together, and the only thing that came close to making me as happy as that was knowing that we would be home for Christmas.

# CHAPTER 32

Ash

Thirty minutes after sundown, with no sign of the men returning, I'd decided enough was enough, and I needed to call the tree farm where Jake and the guys had planned to go.

"Okay, thank you so much," I told Mrs. Gersbach. "We are indebted to you."

"*Nein, Schatz,*" she responded in German before continuing in English. "It is Christmas Eve, and we wish you well."

I smiled at the kindness everyone in this beautiful town had shown us since we arrived, even after the guys made a mockery of the Nativity scene.

"All right," I said, walking into the sitting room of this grand chalet. "You girls either aren't going to believe this, or it won't surprise you at all."

"They got lost?" Nat laughed and looked at Addy, continuing their card game. "Go fish, cutey pie."

"Oh, God," Avery said. "Why didn't they call us?"

"Because, as I suspected, no one took their cell phones," I chuckled. "Most importantly, Mrs. Gersbach said the men don't want us to know their sleigh broke and that they were rescued walking in snowshoes, *each of them leading a reindeer.*"

"Of course, they don't," Laney chuckled. "I can see it now, Jim and Spencer excitedly filling us in on how Jake and Collin finally fucked up their Christmas extravaganza."

"Knowing them, they won't want us to know their sorry butts were rescued five miles away from the house. Who knows? There's a good reason for it?"

"It's called *pride*," Carmen stated with annoyance.

"I figured you'd be more sympathetic because Dad and John are out there at the mercy of Jake and Collin?" I said to my stepmom.

"Oh, no," Carmen said sassily. "I have no sympathies for a man who chooses to go along with the games to cover up a serious, potentially life-threatening situation." Then she sighed, "The only one I might feel sorry for is my grandson, but if he goes along with this cover-up, he gets no sympathy from Abuelita."

"Well, I agree with Carmen," Nat chimed in. "And we fuck with—" She stopped herself and covered Addy's hand after she cussed, "Sorry, honey. Aunt Nat didn't mean to throw out the mother of all curse words."

"You know who my mom is, right?" Addy said with a laugh since everyone knew the F-word was Avery's favorite.

"Excellent point," Nat said. "Now, why don't we ladies be the ones to end this little war that's been going on since we left the Maldives?"

"Well, if we're being technical, it *started* when we arrived in the Maldives," Laney said.

"It doesn't matter. Eventually, all this nonsense caught up with every single one of them," Nat said. "And I say it's time we get some straight answers about what happened to the sleigh and find out why no one was smart enough to carry a phone for safety purposes."

"Agreed," Carmen stated. "This could've been very bad. What if they weren't found until it was too late? No, I won't let them get away with acting like nothing happened."

"You're right. They think they're going to waltz up here as if nothing happened?" Avery added. "It's typical of them."

"Totally typical," I chuckled. "I guess I should've known this would always end with us putting them in their places."

"As it should always be," Nat teased. "Now, what exactly did Mrs. Gersbach say to you?"

"Well, she told the men that we called to ask the Gersbachs if they could go looking for them because we were worried," I started. "And after they were rescued, they insisted that she call me back to tell me nothing had happened, and nothing went wrong. So, being the upright woman she is, she immediately told me the truth instead of their tale."

"Women always looking out for each other, right?" Avery said, shaking her head at the bullshit the guys were attempting to pull. "And the only reason they're pretending everything is perfectly fine is because they know they screwed up, and it could've been much worse."

"As if we wouldn't notice they have no tree? That wouldn't be a dead giveaway that something went wrong?" Laney questioned.

"They paid a pretty high price to get the largest tree on site and for a group of people to come here and decorate it. They probably told them some sad story about how they weren't going to have Christmas Eve now that they've missed everything because of their broken sleigh," I answered.

Carmen rolled her eyes, "They are smug bastards who want to keep this concealed for fear of embarrassment."

"I can't wait until we drag it out of them," Nat said.

"Maybe it's petty on our part," I started, "but I think it's a perfect way to end it all."

"Hearing the men try to lie through their teeth and defend themselves in this situation is enough for me," Nat said with a smile. "We need to play dumb and drag it out of them that way. We'll start with how everything was perfect on Christmas Eve until our men weren't home in time. They'll ruin it from there with their lies and excuses, and eventually, they'll be caught and have to admit they screwed up."

"We start with the Christmas tree," Avery said, "and go from there."

"I still can't believe they've convinced *other people* to decorate *our* tree, which was supposed to be the big, family Christmas crescendo," I added.

"I was looking forward to that, too," Carmen winked. "It's a shame they changed that part of the festive Christmas plans after having it in motion all week."

"Quite the shame," Nat added to the mischievous spirit escalating in the room. "I was *so* looking forward to singing carols around the tree and decorating it while holding hands with Spence."

As we decided our next move, we saw the men coming up the driveway in a van, pulling a trailer with a massive tree. I covered my mouth and smiled when I saw another van pull in behind them, and a large group of cheerful people stepped out.

"Looks like they're all here, tree decorators and all," I said.

"Time to switch up the game," Nat said. "Now, let's watch these lying little holiday elves cough up the truth about breaking sleighs and getting stranded in the woods until *we* sent out help for them."

I guess this was bound to happen in the end. We saved the men, and they were too damn arrogant to show gratitude for it. Instead, they chose to lie and have others deceive us before daring to admit anything went wrong.

It was petty, but everyone who knew our husbands could understand.

Once we stepped out of the house and heard *all the men*, not just Jake and Collin, singing *Blue Christmas,* we knew it was time to settle the score.

# CHAPTER 33

❄

Jake

*Five minutes before pulling up to the chalet...*

Thank God Mrs. Gersbach went along with our little white lie and informed Ash that we were all fine and good. We didn't want to lie to our wives on Christmas Eve—of all the nights—but we also didn't want them to know we'd nearly screwed up the whole thing either.

Ultimately, it was determined that the women were enjoying the festivities far too much for us to ruin it with a tiny little mess-up, most notably, not behaving like the responsible adults we were supposed to be and bringing our phones.

Ah, who am I kidding? We voted unanimously not to tell the women because we'd fucked up massively, and no one wanted to get

THE HOLIDAYS WITH DR. MITCHELL

drilled for it. We'd banded together to save our egos, especially because the ladies had saved our asses by calling the tree farm to see if we were okay.

"All right, everyone knows where we go from here?" I said, turning around from the front seat and eyeing the rest of the pathetic pack of wannabe alpha males sitting in the back two rows in this van.

"You think singing some Christmas carols will distract them from the fact that we hired a crew to decorate a tree we purchased?" Jim asked, arching an eyebrow at me.

"I'm beginning to think you're only going along with this idea because you want to watch me and Collin *finally* fuck it up," I said.

Jim smirked as he eyed Spencer, sitting next to him in the back row, then returned his relaxed expression to me. "That's exactly why I'm going along with it and have offered zero advice about how to ensure the women don't find out that your festive sleigh ride into the middle of the Alps didn't end in disaster," he chuckled.

"Zero advice, eh?" Collin quipped. "What do you call your statement when we hired people to help us decorate the stupid tree?"

"Right," I answered. "I think you said that if we allow the women to believe we hired these people, they won't ask questions because it showed we were doting on them and the kids."

"They're not wrong," Spencer said to Jim. "You're the one who added to this nonsensical scheme to save your ass, too."

"What can I say?" Jim smirked. "I'm in the mood for bourbon with a splash of eggnog and watching my three best ladies enjoy their Christmas Eve. I'd hate for them to waste it watching me kick my brother's ass."

"All of you can say what you will, but this plan is doomed," Mark said. "Carmen will see right through our scheme, and we will end up looking like cowardly fools for not showing gratitude to the women for saving our behinds," he said with a laugh while ruffling the top of John's head.

"Do you think Grandma Carm will find out?" John cringed.

"Not if your dad and uncles are convincing enough," Mark looked out the window as the van pulled into the driveway. "Singing *Blue Christmas* might help us, though," he smiled at me. "That sassy vixen loves Elvis Presley."

I grinned and rubbed my hands together, "Then, the plan is to stay the course and give these beautiful wives and children of ours the best Christmas Eve ever."

"Santa might not come if we *lie to the people we love* on Christmas Eve," Jim taunted.

I eyed my son, who stopped believing in Santa years ago because the idea of a man traversing the world in one night didn't make sense to his logical brain. "Nice try, Uncle Jim," I said. "John's too old for those silly threats."

"Uncle Jim is right, Dad," John said. "If mom finds out you're lying to her to save your butt, I'm pretty sure it's *really* going to be a Blue Christmas."

"You listen to Uncle Jimmy too much, John," I said. "He lives his life playing defense with paranoia, but your dad and Uncle Collin don't think like that."

"Well, we're about to see if *Uncle Jimmy* is right or wrong because we've all decided to keep the truth from the ladies tonight, and they're walking out of the house to greet us. Let's hope this Christmas Carol nonsense saves Christmas," Spencer said.


WE STEPPED out of the van, and Collin and I instantly busted out in song while the people we hired to bring in the tree and set it up in the grand living room bustled around. From the looks of them, we even amplified their moods and Christmas Spirit with all our festiveness and singing.

I had no idea what they truly thought of us weirdos, but I'm sure we were making a statement.

"Jake," Ash said with a smile before focusing on John. "Hi, sweetheart. Look at you," she said, hugging our son, making me instantly feel guilty for having him lie to his mother. "Did you have fun?"

"I did," John answered.

"And what's the meaning behind you singing *Blue Christmas?*" Nat questioned.

Her calculating expression threw me off a bit, but Nat was never a match for me and my wit when it came to things like this.

"Simple," I smiled cheerfully at her while Ash went with John to see our Christmas tree. "The fact that you ladies had to call the Christmas Tree Farm to check on us showed us that you were lonely and *having a Blue Christmas* without us. It played perfectly into the reasons why we were running late."

"Which are?" Carmen questioned. Now I really was off step because I didn't want to lie to her and have her delicious tamales taken away from me for the upcoming year.

"Huh?" I questioned, my moral compass beginning to spin out of control.

"Why are you late, Jacob?" she asked. "You just said there were *reasons.*"

I blinked, totally frozen by the thought of tamale deprivation of all things.

"The reasons are what he just told you," Mark said, coming to my defense, "because we wanted to be able to sing your favorite Christmas song."

Carmen eyed Mark as if searching his soul for the truth, and something told me that the women were onto us.

"Is that so?" she offered. "Well, I can't say I'm upset about that part, but I am upset that you're late."

"We plan to make up for that, but let's get into the house because I'm freezing my ass off," Collin said, running interference because he'd also noticed that our ship might be sunk already.

"QUESTION," Avery said, turning to Jim where they sat. "What happened to all of us decorating the tree together?"

We'd only been in the house for twenty minutes, warming up in the large living room and listening to Christmas music, which was beefing up the Christmas vibe so much so that, fifteen minutes ago, I thought we were off the hook. Naturally, I should've known better. This was another hurdle we would have to jump, but we were prepared for it.

The only question now was whether Jim could hold his own against his wife. I looked at him, seeing his expression grow somber, and I knew my brother was going to stay the course.

"Ask Jake or Collin. That part was their idea," he deflected immediately.

"So?" Avery eyed me.

The thing about lying to cover up being a jackass was that you had to stack one lie on top of another lie. Gone were the days when I was polished and actively practicing this art form. Since I'd become a happily married man, settling down and keeping no secrets from my beloved, I'd had no need for such skills. I had to dig deep into my old ways to keep up this façade and then pray the women got drunk on eggnog so the interrogation would end.

"The truth is," I looked at Jim and then at Spencer. Everyone but the kids, who were helping the staff decorate the tree, was quietly waiting for me to speak. "Forget it. I hate to say it because I don't want to ruin Christmas."

"Go ahead, baby," my wife offered with a mischievous grin. "I'm sure there's no way you could ruin Christmas after everything you guys have done to make it the perfect holiday."

"I'll say it," Collin said. "Jim and Spence were bitching that they would have to decorate a Christmas tree after their prissy little fingernails got dirty while cutting down the tree we searched far and wide to find."

"Exactly," I said, mildly thrown off because I could tell my wife saw through my bullshit, "and so, as a peace offering and a Christmas Eve gift, we decided to let them off the hook."

"Jim was going on and on, and Spencer was whining just the same," Collin continued. "And Jake and I said it was a sorry way to take away from all of the Christmas cheer we'd created for everyone, but we told them we'd let Jim hire tree decorators so—"

"So, I could spend the evening with my beautiful wife and daughters," Jim interrupted Collin.

"You're the best man ever," Avery said, caressing Jim's face and kissing his lips. "Thank you for thinking about us like that."

Collin and I eyed each other, watching Jim get off the hook without trying. For some reason, Laney and Ash's reproachful stares told me we wouldn't be so lucky.

"I still don't understand why we needed to hire anyone to decorate the Christmas tree?" Nat pressed. "It would've been fine without the additional decorations, and we already have decorated trees in every room of this house, including the kitchen."

*"On the first day of Christmas, my true love gave to me..."* Collin busted into song.

*"A partridge in a pear tree,"* I added.

"Nice soprano, buddy," Collin said, raising his glass in the hope that his sudden outburst of song would derail the questioning women.

I raised my glass in response. "Thanks, man. I learned from the best, you."

"All right, I'm *completely done* with the Christmas singing of it all," Ash said in annoyance. "If one of you doesn't tell us the *truth* about what happened tonight, all of you will be singing about your Blue Christmas in another place."

"Ash, it's all part of the—"

"Oh, no, it isn't," Laney gave herself away with a giggle. "Tell us what happened and who broke the sleigh," she looked at Collin.

"Not me," he held both hands up. "It was John," he pointed at my innocent son hanging ornaments with the other children.

"John?" Jim said with a laugh.

"You're blaming *John* because you and Jakey thought bringing a sleigh over unpacked snow would be a good idea, causing its runner to break?" Spencer added.

I narrowed my eyes at the scene unfolding, knowing that this joke was about to be on Collin and me if we didn't find some way out of this.

"You know something?" I said, smiling, standing, and walking to where my wife sat with a questioning expression on the sofa. "We're merely trying not to look like a bunch of dipshits for nearly screwing up Christmas."

"So, you lied and blamed an innocent child when the truth came out?" Nat said with a laugh.

"That's why I'm ending all this here and now. I admit that Collin and I weren't fully aware we could damage the sleigh by bringing it off the packed road and through the forest," I said.

"I can't tell you how much of a relief it is not to hear a Christmas carol from you whilst admitting that," Nat said with a laugh, comfortably sitting on her husband's lap in an oversized chair.

"Well, it's because the payback is over. Now, we can get back to our old ways of spending the holidays," Collin said. "You know, boring and unmotivated for Christmas pleasantries."

"As long as there's no more singing," Spencer added.

"Yeah, okay. It's over. Merry Christmas Eve, everyone," I said, knowing that even though it came to a bumpy end, the women had loved our way of bringing in holiday-themed activities based on Christmas tunes...at least, that's what I hoped. Being insufferably cheesy with the songs for a week certainly wasn't easy.

"No," Jim said. "It's not over yet."

I held my hands up. "It's been exhausting, but now, everyone can return to their seasonal Christmas festivities the good old-fashioned way, by drinking eggnog, watching television, and opening a present on Christmas Eve."

"We'll put the kids to bed," Collin said, leading everyone down a depressed and boring road just to get them all to admit that this was the best Christmas holiday they'd ever spent with friends and family. "Then we can enjoy a little Christmas cheer while everyone delights in opening gifts tomorrow and pigging out on food so badly that we all go into food comas for the rest of the day."

I smiled, seeing the expressions on everyone's faces starting to change, "And you all get Christmas back the way you're used to it."

"I'm not ashamed to admit that I've enjoyed all of this, even the silly Christmas songs," Carmen shockingly admitted. "The kids have been happy and engaged all week, and seeing them participate in all the thoughtful activities has been a delight. I don't think I've ever been in the Christmas spirit more than I have on this wonderfully crazy trip," she chuckled.

"I say we keep my bride happy," Mark chirped, "and keep these Christmas celebrations going like we have all week."

"Agreed," Ash concurred. "Even though it's been crazy, this has been the most exciting and hilarious Christmas I've ever had." She stood up and walked over to me, "And it's all because you and Collin couldn't let it rest that those boys played a prank on the two of you."

"All of you are very welcome," I said. "Now, who wants to play Santa's Christmas Eve elf and start passing out the Christmas Eve presents?"

My son immediately turned, and the boy, who was usually consumed by electronics and anything other than his family on Christmas Eve, was thrilled to be Santa's helper. Knowing that my son had enjoyed this trip to the fullest made me grateful for what I had to endure to put these things in motion.

Sure, we heightened the festivities with Christmas tunes, a perfect and beautiful Swiss Chalet, sleighs, and reindeer, but even when all that material stuff was out of sight, John seemed a little lighter and happier. He'd experienced the true gift of Christmas: being happy, silly, and carefree with the family and friends you love.

I could finally see and fully embrace that life is better lived when you're with your loved ones, doing crazy and extremely silly things— even if you are at war with your brother while you're doing it. We were the most fortunate group of best friends in the world, not because we were spoiled with wealth but because we were always there for each other no matter what.

Gifts came in many different forms, and my greatest gift came from the happiness and good health of the people I loved most.

Jim stood and raised his glass after the Christmas Eve presents were opened. "To the best Christmas week *ever*," he smiled at me, "and to the eternal goofballs who made it all happen." Everyone sipped their drinks, and Jim finished by looking at the children. "Are you kids ready for Santa?"

"Yes," they all proclaimed in unison.

"Then, it's time I conclude this night by electing the one who will read *'Twas the night before Christmas*," Jim said. He was always the one to read the story since he liked to do voices, but tonight, he was passing the torch. "Mark, would you do the honors?"

"I'd love to," Mark said, looking like he'd just won an award.

I couldn't imagine a better group of friends to celebrate this holiday with. There was nowhere else I'd rather be.

*Merry Christmas to All, and to All a Good Night...*

Ash

I LAY IN BED, nestled tightly to Jake's side, watching the snowfall. Large flakes floated like feathers, dancing in the chilly breeze, and I listened to the fire crackling in the fireplace, appreciating this beautiful Christmas Card view of the Alps.

"Good morning, angel," Jake said, rousing awake and turning to face me.

I draped my leg over his perfectly polished and sexually satiated body, moving him closer to me and gaining a soft kiss on my forehead.

"Merry Christmas to King of all Christmas festivities," I chuckled.

*"Frohe Weihnachten,"* he said in his cute morning voice.

"Oh?" I said, running my fingertips over his forehead. "I didn't realize you'd been polishing your German. Care to translate?"

"*Actually*, it's Swiss German dialect, and it means Merry Christmas," he said, pretending to be pretentious.

"You sure are sexy with that second language you've picked up."

"Well, I'm not fluent in four languages like my brother, but I've spent enough time being rescued from frostbite on a Swiss Christmas tree farm to learn a thing or two," he laughed. "For all the time we spent in Europe with my dad, you'd think more of the languages would've stuck, but hey. I rarely have to speak Italian or French when I'm performing open-heart surgery, so it's just as well I let Jim focus on that."

"Well, I'm happy you grew up experiencing so many other countries and cultures, even if you never learned the languages," I smiled, loving when Jake reminisced on the fond memories of his past. "You know, we should look into getting a vacation home over here."

"Well, it's not so easy to buy a residential property in Switzerland if you aren't a citizen, but I've considered looking at other places from time to time. I never imagined my lovely wife would care to have anything like that, though."

"It does seem kind of foolish to bring it up after all the beautiful lessons we've all learned this Christmas," I said.

"What, that money and material possessions don't buy happiness?" he laughed.

"Exactly," I chuckled. "Maybe I'm just caught up in this peaceful bubble we've been in here, and I don't want to leave?"

"Baby, it's okay to desire things that you're capable of having," Jake said, "and I know you well enough to know that buying a second home overseas isn't the key to your happiness. We have more than enough money to make that happen; in fact, I would love to have a place where we can take our kids whenever we feel like it. My brother and I loved vacationing in Europe with my dad. It was a bonding experience that kept us close."

"So, it was like a foundation for you two?"

"I guess you could say that, yeah," he said. "Now, if we were to decide on a place, where would you want it to be?"

"Well, I love the English countryside where Jim and Avery have their little castle estate," I toyed with the idea.

"We could purchase a place near them and be neighbors. My brother will hate it," he chuckled.

"Oh, please. He would *not* hate it," I nudged Jake in his ribs playfully. "What about you? What were you thinking of?"

"I'd choose Italy," he said casually.

"Italy?"

"Yeah, I'm a sucker for pasta and fine wines."

I laughed, loving that my husband and I could have silly conversations first thing in the morning on a perfect Christmas day. We probably wouldn't pull the trigger on a second home in Europe, but talking about it and listening to each other's preferences was fun.

It had been a rough year for me, feeling lonely and distanced from the man I loved, but I felt renewed in our love again, and all it took was a solid break from the hustle and bustle of life and a good dose of family and friends to remind us of where our focus should be.

Work had a way of owning every one of us, rich and poor alike. Everyone was in their own private rat race, and if we didn't take time to stop and recharge our batteries, we could be consumed by it. Having an amazing husband to kiss me goodbye every time he left the house was worth more to me than the ability to purchase a second home. Having children who loved and appreciated everything we did for them, big or small, was something you couldn't put a price tag on.

"I see you're thinking about *exactly* what kind of English manor you'd like to purchase?" Jake said, interrupting my quiet thoughts.

I kissed his lips and ran my hand down his side, "No, I'm thinking that all of that would be wonderful, but I'm happy and content with having just this."

He pulled my hand over his dick and smiled, "You mean this?"

"That too," I chuckled, then hugged him. "I love you, Jacob. Thank you for making this the most memorable and festive holiday I could've ever asked for."

"And I'd do it all over again, too, angel," he said, becoming more serious.

"I'm sure you would, especially because it was all based on you giving your brother hell for the last couple of weeks," I chuckled when his lips captured my bottom one.

"Well, that too," he said, running his hand along my cheek. "Honestly, I enjoyed all of it. Seeing Kaley so happy and giggling at every silly thing we did just melted my heart. Her cute little angelic voice singing the Christmas carols she didn't even know until now was probably the cutest thing I've ever seen," he grinned sweetly. "And John? That kid amazes me. I'm so proud and thankful that he got the most out of the experience. For a kid his age to look around and notice that he was enjoying this so much because of who he was with instead of what he would receive means the world to me. All I've ever wanted is for him to grow up knowing that all this money means nothing if you aren't surrounded by people you love and who love you in return, and he understood it this week."

My heart always skipped a beat every time he spoke so sincerely. "You're a wonderful example to him and a tremendous father to them both," I said, drawing closer to him.

"No, baby," he said, his amorousness growing at the same pace as mine. "You're the best wife a man could ask for and the most loving mom our kids could ever dream of having."

Jake's lips went to my neck while he parted my legs with his knee, allowing him access to the one thing that was aching for more of him.

*Knock! Knock! Bang! Bang! Knock!*

"Hold on, Collin," Jake growled, stopping us from going further.

"Daddy, it's Kaley! Santa came, Santa came! You have to come and see!"

"I suddenly forgot it was Christmas morning," I chuckled. "Come on, let's go," I said, scrambling to get out of bed and pulling on my Christmas jammies and robe while Jake did the same.

Before I got to the door, where our impatient daughter stood banging away on it, Jake pulled me into his arms for another kiss, "Last night was incredible, but tonight, we're going to make up for what we just missed out on and then some."

"I'll hold you to it," I teased. "Merry Christmas, lover."

Now, it was time to embrace the holiday traditions of opening gifts, but this year, I knew that I would see it from a different perspective and with a more grateful and happy heart.

This is what Christmas was truly about—love, cheer, happiness, and gifts given from the heart.

*Merry Christmas!*

# EPILOGUE

❄

*(Because we all deserve a Merry Christmas <u>and</u> a Happy New Year...)*

Jake

You didn't think this would end with some cheesy version of us all singing Christmas carols by the candlelit tree in a beautiful chalet in the middle of the Swiss Alps, did you?

No. Not even close.

It was New Year's Eve, and I was back to work after what seemed like having a month off. Lucky for me, my gorgeous wife decided to join me for lunch at the hospital. After lunch, I took her to the private room connected to my office, where I slept when I worked twenty-four-hour shifts, and we got busy like we did in the days before we had kids.

"I love you, baby," I said as she double-checked her outfit, ensuring her clothes and hair appeared just as crisp and perfectly fashioned as they were when she met me for lunch. "And hey, we should do these impromptu lunches more often, eh? It's like back in the old days."

"You had way too much fun in the Alps, Dr. Mitchell," she laughed.

"I had way too much fun torturing my brother if that's what you mean." I reached out to her to lead her out of my office. "Come here," I said, not wanting her to leave. I kissed her neck and inhaled the spicy vanilla perfume John had hunted down as the perfect fragrance to buy his mother for Christmas. "Consider our vows renewed after the way your sexy ass has me performing these days."

"It does feel like old days, doesn't it?" she said with an adorable smile that reminded me of when we first met, making me want to bring her back into my on-call room and ravish her body again.

"You have no idea. Happy New Year, my love," I said. "Tell John to keep his Uncle Jim out of my thirty-year-old, single malt Macallan while I'm working, and he is enjoying the company of the rest of our friends who aren't on-call tonight."

"You know Jim will drink that if he sees it," she said.

"Well, the decoy bottle that I assume he'll go for is set out for the old man, so I hope he indulges himself in that one," I chuckled.

"Jake?" Ash arched an eyebrow at me. "It's New Year's Eve, as in making resolutions about not playing silly pranks on everyone around you."

"That's one New Year resolution I will *never* make, and if my brother thinks I did, and he dares to raid my expensive liquor cabinet?"

"What did you spike it with? Tell me now, in case I'm foolish enough to touch your booze."

"Yeah, you'll want to stay away from that scotch," I warned, nodding at the office secretary, who walked by with a humorous smile.

She must've seen the decorations I'd put up in Stone's office this morning.

"What's in it?"

"Let's just say Jimmy wasn't so discreet with the videos of Collin and me shitting our lives away in those woods, and when I returned to find Dr. Stone was amused by that, it just made me think of one final retaliation move that needed to be done on those who fucked with Collin and me."

Ash rolled her eyes, "What other booze did you tamper with?"

"Just the scotch," I said, pulling on my lab coat and preparing to head to the ER, where I'd spend my time this New Year's Eve with Collin, Cameron Brandt, and John Aster.

"Jake, you've got something else up your sleeve," Ash said, knowing me well.

"Well, Collin laced the figs that Spence, Alex, and Jim love so much because they're fucking weirdos. I wasn't going to say anything because those smug assholes like to eat those while amusing themselves with cigars and cognac, and everyone else stays away from them."

"So, you were willing to take a chance that the kids wouldn't?"

I rolled my eyes. "Eat *figs*? Uh, no, I wasn't worried about that. The kids hate that shit."

"What's in them?"

"Laxatives, no biggie," I said. "Injected them, so they'll be none the wiser."

"So, that's what we're all dealing with? Jim, Alex, and Spence shitting their brains out all night...at *our* house?"

"They need to feel what Collin and I felt in those woods. They had way too much fun doing all the Christmas gags. The retaliation just wasn't over yet," I said. When I leaned down to kiss her, she moved her face away from mine.

All I could do was laugh and love this woman for everything she put up with, having me as a husband and father of her kids.

"I swear our son acts older than you sometimes," she said in disbelief and humor.

"Our son acts just like his Uncle Jim. He needs these candid moments to keep him young, or he'll be gray by the time he reaches high school."

"Hey, nutcracker," Collin said, leaning into his nutcracker prank as if it hadn't gotten old yet to put a life-sized wooden statue in front of my office every Christmas season to keep everyone in the building humored. "Hey, Ash. Are you going to let the kids host everyone tonight so you can hang out with Jake and me for New Year's?"

"I'm thinking this might be the safer bet," Ash said, then hugged Collin. "Happy New Year's. I'm taking off just in case this is the night one of the ladies or kids gets a craving for wild figs."

"Oh, shit. You told her? You can never tell the wives. That's our number one rule," Collin taunted.

"Oh, really? I didn't realize this was some club you both had going?" Ash said.

"It's only so no one gives away their bullshit," Stone walked up, wearing scrubs and most likely hunting me down to join him in the cardiac ER wing. "Nice work, both of you," he eyed Collin and me.

"What did they do to you?" Ash questioned.

"Nothing out of the ordinary for these two," he said. "Luckily, I got laid as a result of it."

"Jesus. You guys are all beyond me. I don't even want to know," Ash said, then offered me a quick kiss and wished us all a Happy New Year before she left the office.

"How did you get laid because of that?" Collin questioned.

"Oh, I don't know. Perhaps it was the blown-up, blue ball ornament with the lyrics to Blue Christmas written on it that you set up outside my office and your clown message, telling everyone I hadn't been laid, so the ornament was dedicated to me? You know, because I'm supposed to have blue balls, I guess?"

"Most women find it pathetic when a loser such as yourself doesn't get laid over the holidays?" I said.

"And most women aren't turned on by Elvis unless they're eighty," Collin added.

"Turns out, the new Elvis movie has all the ladies drooling over him again, and apparently, when it comes to my sexy ass not getting laid, they lined up in an attempt to help me with that dry spell you both are forever saying I'm having?"

"Sounds about right," I said, and that's when mine and Stone's pagers went off simultaneously.

"Looks like it's go-time for you two studs," Collin said. "Happy New Year's."

"We'll hit you up if it dies down," I chuckled, knowing how crazy this night could get in the ER.

And it did. Even so, we enjoyed our New Year's Eve, knowing our families were happy, safe, and celebrating together. In our own special way, we were too. We just did it by saving lives.


Ash


THE THING about the holidays is that they could either bring out the best in us or the worst. It was all determined by your outlook, and since I didn't want to deal with the worst of any situation tonight, especially where my toilets were concerned, I decided I needed to intervene on Jake's final bit of payback.

"I can't believe those little shits were *still* plotting revenge," Alex said as everyone sat around eating the New Year's Eve Chinese food I had catered.

"Shit being the operative word," Bree laughed.

"I'm just glad Ash called ahead and had John remove all the items *laced* with Collin and Jake's special additive," Jim said with a chuckle. "You saved our asses, sis."

"Quite literally," Spencer said, annoyed that Jake and Collin were like ruthless little brothers who didn't know when to quit.

"Well, there's a good lesson here, and I'm thankful to have learned it without having been a part of it," Titus Hawk, the newest and liveliest member of our crazy gang, added.

"What's that, brother?" Jim mused.

"You know exactly what that is," Titus grinned. The man was most certainly a lady killer with his smooth voice and topaz eyes that glittered with his beaming smile. "That I will never join in on pranks to attempt to put Jake and Collin in their places."

"True that," Jim said with a laugh. "Lucky for you, they know you had no idea of our devious intentions when you donated the property for our private use. Not that you aren't a fan of a good prank, but we knew this one would come with retribution from them that you didn't deserve."

"Not yet, anyway." Titus raised his glass and laughed, "Regardless, good looking out, my friends."

"No problem. We put too many years of personal vendettas into that prank to put you in that kind of danger," Spencer said with amusement, having just taken a sip of his drink. "You know those two will keep this going until the end of time, and who are their favorite victims?"

"None other than us," Alex said with an arch of his eyebrow.

"Wait a minute," I said, looking at Spencer. "Where did you get that drink? Is that scotch?"

"Yeah," he said, eyeing his glass. "It's from the *good* liquor cabinet Jake has hidden in his office," he smirked and took a hefty gulp. "My second glass and I already feel that this night will be the best New Year's ever."

"Oh no! Oh shit," I reflexively pulled the glass from him to stop him from taking another victory sip. "That's where I had John put that bottle that Jake spiked with laxatives."

"You had your kid hide the booze? How very alcoholic of you," Titus teased while I stared at Spencer in fear.

"Yeah, well, I had no other option," I sighed. "I called John and told him to throw out the figs Aunt Laney sent over earlier and then move that bottle to his dad's office."

"Why did you raid Jake's office liquor cabinet?" Jim questioned with a laugh.

"Because that's where that asshole always hides the good stuff when we attend parties at his house, and he's at work," Spencer answered. "And I'm still stuck in the days when Jakey would tell us *what's mine is yours...*"

"Well, if you drank enough of that," I said with a laugh, "you're going to feel his pain when it becomes yours and you're shitting your brains out all night like they were at Titus's resort."

"Meh, I'm not too worried about it," he answered. "I don't feel anything out of the norm."

"You better not fuck up my plans for ringing in the New Year with you," Nat looked at Spencer with a fair amount of fury. "If my new lingerie isn't put to proper use after that ball drops tonight, I'll make you suffer far more than diarrhea ever could."

"Weaponizing sex again, lover?" Spencer winked at Nat.

I could instantly tell the man was feeling *more* than just one or two glasses of scotch.

"Um, Spence?" I spoke. "I think you're closer to drunk than you realize. You're probably not going to feel it coming."

"He's fine, Ash," Jim said.


MIDNIGHT WAS FINALLY NEARING after going through rounds of adult card and board games while the kids played upstairs in the game room. We finally turned on the television to watch the ball drop, and then we went outside to watch fireworks get set off from the ocean barge that Mitchell and Associates had hired for everyone in Malibu to enjoy.

Everything was going perfectly until the laxative finally caught up to Spencer, who let out a howl like a dying coyote as he ran to the nearest bathroom with his butt cheeks clenched so hard that he looked two inches shorter.

"Well, looks like Spence is going to miss the fireworks," Jim mused with a smirk.

"Sounds like he's going to have plenty of those going off in that bathroom," I said, shaking my head. "Can we all agree that pranking Collin and Jake—or at least trying to get them back—is never a good idea?"

Alex grinned at me, "Sweetheart, this war between us has gone on for years. The only reason Jim and I aren't shitting our brains out in the closest bathroom is because we *know* better."

"Exactly, we've dealt with those two since childhood, but after tonight, Spence will know not to be so trusting around Jake or Collin in the early days after pranking their asses as well as we did."

"The early days," Nat questioned with an arch of her eyebrow. "It's been almost a month of this?"

"Yeah, it usually takes a good six months with no activity to begin trusting those two again," Jim advised.

"Let's get the kids downstairs. I don't want them to miss the fireworks," Avery said, returning our attention to the New Year's celebration.

Even though I tried to run interference and save someone's literal ass tonight, Spence fell victim. Maybe that would be enough for my husband and Collin to calm their butts down for a while?

Probably not.

This had been a full-circle holiday, and although I was thankful for all my friends and family, I was exhausted and ready to curl up in bed. The new year had started a little over an hour ago, and I planned to go into it refreshed, renewed, and restored.

Overall, it was a beautiful holiday; I would cherish it forever, and our children would never forget it. I loved my life, my husband, my children, and family and friends, and I was excited to see where the new year would take all of us.

The End

# SPECIAL NOTE FROM THE AUTHOR

*Wishing you all a wonderful safe holiday season and a very Merry Christmas...[without pranks, of course ;)] However you celebrate, I hope this year is filled with joy, happiness and absolute fulfillment!*

*I am truly blessed and thankful to have each and everyone of you trusting my writing and reading these books that I have an absolute blast writing for you.*

*Going into the New Year, I have so many exciting ideas and plans for my writing and I hope you all will continue to follow me on this amazing journey that I'm beyond grateful to be on.*

*I love each and every one of you and can't thank you enough for being such an amazing support for me.*

*Xoxo,*

*Raylin*

**_Updates for future books..._**

I'm so thankful for each and every one of you and am excited to say that I will be continuing on with the Billionaires' Club series, releasing one or two books in it every year and up until I run out of fun love stories to share with our sexy alpha and doctor men. So, keep an eye on this series and follow me on Amazon, Facebook, or BookBub to be alerted when preorders go up or new books are released.

Also, I plan to start writing fun and exciting short stories from each of our favorite couples in the Billionaires' Club series as well. These will come in the form of Romantic Holiday short stories (like this one) and will help us all keep up with the lives that our favorite characters are living in each of their own Happily Ever Afters.

I'm also excited to announce that I will be starting a new sister series, and trilogy of the Hawk Brothers that will stay closely tied in to our Southern California Billionaires [Oh, and East Coast Billionaires…sorry Sebastian ;)] …So be on the look out for preorders for these brothers as they prepare to steal our hearts too.

I have so many exciting plans as I move toward the future with my writing and I hope you all will continue this exciting journey with me.

# ABOUT THE AUTHOR

Raylin Marks is the author of the Billionaires' Club Series. She enjoys writing, adventures, and good wholesome love…in all of that (well, some of that) she orchestrates timeless and exciting romance novels for anyone who dares to read them.

When Raylin Marks is not writing, she's usually found out in nature, either on the shores of California's West Coast, or up in the majestic mountains—somewhere or anywhere out in nature, gathering ideas for a new fun and exciting adventure to write for her readers.

Oh, and yeah, so she drinks too much coffee too.

Keep up with Raylin at any one of the sites below. Oh, P.S., she LOVES her fans, so don't be afraid to contact her personally if you want at: raylinmarks99@gmail.com.

# ALSO BY RAYLIN MARKS

The Books in the Billionaires' Club Series can all be read as standalone and in any order. It's more enjoyable to read them in order as each character is introduced, but not necessary.

Billionaires Club Series:

Dr. Mitchell

Mr. Mitchell

Dr. Brooks

Mr. Grayson

Dr. Brandt

Mr. Monroe

Dr. Aster

Mr. Aster

Dr. Stone (Preorder link)

Billionaires' Club Holiday Romance Series

The Holidays with Dr. Mitchell

The Hawk Brothers (Links available once preorders are live in the Amazon store. These announcements will be made via: Newsletter, Facebook, and Instagram.

I'm trying to get TikTok down, so every now and then I will play over there and try to update, but I'm not very up to date with it all yet LOL.

Printed in Great Britain
by Amazon

55859280R00119